Harvey
Comes
Home

Harvey
Comes
Home

by **COLLEEN NELSON**

Illustrations by Tara Anderson

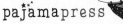
paj**a**mapress

First published in Canada and the United States in 2019

Text copyright © 2019 Colleen Nelson
Illustration copyright © 2019 Tara Anderson
This edition copyright © 2019 Pajama Press Inc.
This is a first edition.

10 9 8 7 6 5 4 3 2 1

www.pajamapress.ca   info@pajamapress.ca

The publisher gratefully acknowledges the support of the Canada Council for the Arts and the Ontario Arts Council for its publishing program. We acknowledge the financial support of the Government of Canada through the Canada Book Fund (CBF) for our publishing activities.

Library and Archives Canada Cataloguing in Publication

Title: Harvey comes home / by Colleen Nelson ; illustrated by Tara Anderson.
Names: Nelson, Colleen, author. | Anderson, Tara, illustrator.
Description: First edition.
Identifiers: Canadiana 20190050632 | ISBN 9781772780970 (hardcover)
Classification: LCC PS8627.E555 H37 2019 | DDC jC813/.6—dc23

Publisher Cataloging-in-Publication Data (U.S.)

Names: Nelson, Colleen, author. | Anderson, Tara, illustrator.
Title: Harvey Comes Home / Colleen Nelson.
Description: Toronto, Ontario Canada : Pajama Press, 2019. | Summary: "A young boy volunteering at a retirement home finds a stray dog and notices that it revives decades-old memories for a bitter resident. The boy bonds with the resident as he listens to stories about growing up in Saskatchewan during the Great Depression. Thanks to his new friend and his canine companion, the elderly man is able to pass away peacefully, immersed in fond memories of his youth"— Provided by publisher.
Identifiers: ISBN 978-1-77278-097-0 (hardcover)
Subjects: LCSH: Dogs -- Juvenile fiction. | Retirement communities – Juvenile fiction. | Depressions—1929—Canada – Juvenile fiction. | BISAC: JUVENILE FICTION / Animals / Dogs. | JUVENILE FICTION / Historical / Canada / Post-Confederation (1867–) | JUVENILE FICTION / Social Themes / Adolescence & Coming of Age.
Classification: LCC PZ7.1N457Ha |DDC [F] – dc23

Original art created with graphite pencil on Canson drawing paper
Interior illustrations—Tara Anderson
Cover design—Rebecca Bender
Text design—Lorena Gonzalez Guillen
Cover image—Oscar, running fast © Christopher Walker

Manufactured by Friesens
Printed in Canada

Pajama Press Inc.
181 Carlaw Ave. Suite 251 Toronto, Ontario Canada, M4M 2S1

Distributed in Canada by UTP Distribution
5201 Dufferin Street Toronto, Ontario Canada, M3H 5T8

Distributed in the U.S. by Ingram Publisher Services
1 Ingram Blvd. La Vergne, TN 37086, USA

For
Gordon and *Marie Pickering*
–C.N.

For *Uncle Bruce*
–T.A.

Chapter 1

Harvey

Harvey is a West Highland Terrier; a ratter with a white coat, extra shiny and clean because he was just groomed yesterday. He trots ahead of Maggie, feeling quite smart. He enjoys the chill of the early November air as it rustles against his skin.

Tail held high, ears pricked and nose down low, Harvey follows the scent left by Rosie, another Westie who has been here recently. He lifts his leg and, with a little squirt, adds his scent to a lamppost.

Maggie tugs at the leash, reminding him they are meant to be walking, but all the smells are too distracting. He could spend all day drinking them in at just one lamppost. Not like his yard, where everything is familiar. The only excitement is the squirrels that scamper and race through the treetops, taunting him.

He loves and hates those squirrels. He can't imagine his days without them. Like any good ratter, he watches for them. When he sees one invade his yard, he paws at the door and barks to be let out, desperate to chase it.

So far, on this walk, there have been no squirrels, but the bright smells make up for it. They zip up his nose and into his brain.

Harvey can't see bright colors, but if he could, he would know that Maggie has the most beautiful color of hair. Like a hot metal poker, it glows red, orange, and copper, and curls at the ends. Maggie takes her hair for granted, even though it is the first thing people compliment her on. The hair is from her mother, but the slight build and lanky frame are both from her father. She has a smattering of freckles across her nose, and more appear in the summer. Her eyes are small, but sharp and quizzical, and teachers think of her as the quiet, studious type. Maggie is at an age when a uniform of tights and a long hoodie is worn daily. Her hair is most often tied up in a ponytail. She doesn't care about clothes or boys, at least not yet. She is happiest at home with Harvey.

Harvey never knows what the day will bring with Maggie. Some days she is at home with him and other days she leaves and comes back with a bag layered with so many smells. Harvey could sniff it all day and never catch all the scents. Maggie lugs that bag up to her room. She unzips it and sighs, then sits down to work, pencil scratching and papers flipping. Harvey is content to lie on her bed and watch, pleased that Maggie is home.

But today, something is different. There is a lot of activity when he and Maggie return from their walk. Harvey lets Maggie unclip his leash. He waits by the door, trying to make sense of the hustle and bustle. He sees Maggie's parents, walking with quick, rushed steps and speaking loudly to each other.

The two little girls, twins, who often try to grab Harvey's tail, are being jostled about. Harvey can tell something is going on. There are new smells at the front door, and Harvey goes to inspect them. Besides the usual scents of leather, wool, and outdoor grit, Harvey sniffs out three big things. They are lined up in a row and smell of the damp basement. He catches a whiff of the stuffed bunny from Maggie's room—the one he's not supposed to grab—locked inside one of the cases. What is *it* doing in there? he wonders. He paws at the case and sniffs intently, looking for other trapped scents. He is concentrating so hard that he doesn't know Maggie is behind him until she reaches out and grabs him.

She holds him close to her chest and whispers in his ear. "I love you so much, Harvs. I'm going to miss you!"

Harvey hears the catch in her voice. He pokes his black nose into her face and sees that her eyes sparkle with tears. Harvey licks at her chin, desperate to make sense of all this.

A car pulls up outside. He barks to let everyone know but gets an annoyed "Shush!" from Maggie's father before he's even finished. Harvey takes a few steps forward. Natural curiosity makes his tail point straight in the air as he waits for the door to open. When it does, a girl, taller than his Maggie, steps in. Voices rise with excitement and greeting. Joining the fray, Harvey runs up to welcome the girl, but is gently scolded to stay back.

The new girl holds out her hand for him and crouches down. She's wearing jeans with holes in the knees, so he can smell flowery lotion. He sniffs out her heavy leather boots— the kind of boots he'd love to gnaw on, but knows he can't. Leather boots are his favorite. They hold scents, and the flavor explodes in his mouth, not to mention the sensation on his tongue. Like a good belly rub.

"Hey, Harvey," she says. He likes her voice. It's soft and encouraging. He noses closer, curious.

"Harvey, this is Olivia. She's going to look after you." Maggie uses the same singsong voice he's heard her use with the little girls. His Maggie wants him to like this girl. He'll do anything for his Maggie, so he takes a polite sniff of her hand, likes the smells, and gives it an appreciative lick. The girl's hand darts up to his head and rubs between his ears. Then she stands up.

Harvey isn't ready for the head scratch to be over. He steps closer to her and stands on his hind legs, reaching his front paws up her legs. His nails pull on the denim.

"Harvey!" Maggie's mother admonishes.

He's about to get down, but the girl shakes her head and says, "It's okay." And Harvey is rewarded with another head scratch. He likes this girl. There's no jumping or fidgeting like some of Maggie's other friends. Confident that she poses no threat, Harvey goes to Maggie, who sinks to the floor and gives him a cuddle.

His Maggie. His eyes half-close with contentment.

Maggie's mother leads the girl into the house and chatters to her. He's so comfortable on the tile floor beside Maggie that he almost misses the sound of another car in the driveway.

"Taxi's here," Maggie calls out. But her voice is choked. Harvey turns to face her, tilting his head.

There's a rush to the door. Maggie's father appears from his office and everyone collects together, waiting. Harvey's skin prickles, just like it does when Maggie is sick. Something is going on, something different. Maggie holds him tightly against her chest. He can feel her heart beating and hear her sniffle.

"We're going on a trip, Harvey! Me, Mom, Dad, and the twins. You're staying here with Olivia."

He senses trepidation in her voice and pricks his ears. She rubs his back thoughtfully as her father drags the suitcases outside. Another man helps him, and Harvey yelps, catching a quick whiff of new smells. And then there is more action. Maggie stands up. Jackets are handed out. Twins are wrangled. Maggie's father comes back inside and shouts instructions. Harvey stands on his hind legs and stretches up to Maggie's knees. He needs her attention.

"Bye, Harvey," she says. She zips her jacket and takes hold of the suitcase that has her favorite things trapped inside. Little wheels on the bottom make it roll across the floor.

"Here, Harvey," Olivia calls. He can smell a treat in the air. He isn't sure what he's done to earn it, but he turns to the smell and sniffs it out. It crunches in his mouth. When he turns back, the door is shut and his Maggie has disappeared. Where is she?

He races to the window in the front room that looks out over the driveway. He watches as the taxi departs, stuffed full with his Maggie and her family. He can see her staring back at him. She raises her hand to wave.

And then his Maggie is gone.

Chapter 2
Austin

Charlie, the manager at Brayside Retirement Villa, made it real clear to Grandpa that he wasn't paying me. I could come to Brayside after school, no problem. But if Grandpa thought he'd found me a part-time job, the answer was no.

I bet Grandpa just smiled at Charlie, like he always does, and walked away, whistling. Charlie thinks he runs Brayside, since he's the manager, but without Grandpa, the whole place would fall apart. Grandpa's been the custodian for over sixteen years. Not a thing goes on here that he doesn't know about.

Brayside is a home for old people. There are three floors, and by the time people are moved up to the third floor, they aren't going anywhere else. Grandpa looks after all the floors, but he kept me busy on the first floor, where people still live independently. Thanks to my deal with Grandpa, I provided unpaid labor for the rest of the year.

Well, technically, it wasn't a deal. It was a punishment.

I learned my lesson—honest! And I'm glad it was Grandpa who answered the phone the day the principal called. If Mom had found out I'd been caught with firecrackers in the boys' bathroom, I'd have been scraping gum off the sidewalk or cleaning toilets with my toothbrush.

When Grandpa asked me why I'd tried to light fireworks at school, I lied and told him it was a dare. The real reason was too embarrassing.

But here it is: I thought I would make some friends. Stupid, right? I know that now, but at the time I thought kids would be impressed. It would set me apart, make me cool in my own way. But everything backfired, no pun intended, when the school custodian walked in and found the firecrackers, a lighter—and me. My first and only stunt was a fail. I spent the rest of the day in the principal's office.

It took hours of begging Grandpa not to tell Mom. My main argument was that she'd been through enough and didn't need to know her kid was a screwup too. "You're not a screwup," Grandpa sighed. "You made a mistake."

"That's not how Mom will see it." I guess he figured I had a point, because instead of blabbing to Mom, we made an arrangement. It wouldn't help me get any friends, but Grandpa was convinced an honest day's work would keep me out of trouble. So, after school till six o'clock every Monday to Friday, he put me to work cleaning things that weren't even dirty. Washing windows and dusting, usually. Both of those jobs meant I was standing still or moving slow, which made me easy to talk to. And man, do old people like to talk. Most of them, anyway.

One guy, Mr. Pickering, never said two words since I'd started working at Brayside. To be honest, I was a little afraid of Mr. Pickering. He had a ring of scraggly white hair that circled his head. His face was craggy, like a mountain slope. He might have been tall once, but now he was all stooped and weathered, like an old falling-down house battered by wind and rain.

I asked Grandpa how old he thought Mr. Pickering was. Grandpa tucked his screwdriver into the pocket of his blue coveralls and stood thinking. "He's been here for fifteen years, or close to it. I'm gonna guess ninety-five or ninety-six. Oldest one on the floor, that's for sure."

"Do you think he'll live to be one hundred?" I did the math. If Mr. Pickering was ninety-six, that meant he was born in 1923. "He must've seen a lot."

"Bet he'd tell you, if you asked," Grandpa said.

I doubted that. Mr. Pickering was just one of those people who looked like he was happier to be left alone.

Chapter 3

Harvey

Harvey can't resist squirrels. The next morning, when Olivia lets him out back, he sees one race across the fence, and takes off after it. The squirrel scampers up to safety on the branch of a spruce tree. Harvey waits below, knowing there is nowhere for the squirrel to run except down the trunk. Harvey's nose quivers at the scents of pinecones and sap that fill the air. His tail pokes straight up, alert, as he stares into the dark branches above.

A bird distracts Harvey, and the squirrel seizes his opportunity. He races down the tree trunk and bolts for the fence a few yards away. Harvey tears after it, but the squirrel is faster. It makes it to the fence and races along the top. Usually, Harvey's chase is stymied by the gate that keeps him trapped in the yard. But today, that is not the case. Olivia didn't know to check the latch on the gate, and it has come loose. Harvey, in a blur of white, finds himself in the front yard and hot on the trail of the squirrel. In fact, Harvey chases the squirrel all the way to the end of Maggie's street. The squirrel finally escapes by racing up a tree and jumping onto a roof, where it chatters maddeningly at Harvey from two stories up. Harvey barks at first, but now he is distracted by all the smells. Nose down, he engrosses himself in locating and isolating each one, sprinkling many with his own scent.

He catches a whiff of putrid rubber and tar just before the blast of a horn sends him bolting out of the way. His heart beats wildly in his chest. Harvey knows that streets are dangerous places. The loud, rumbling beasts that chug up and down them are to be avoided. Harvey keeps running through yards and thickets of trees.

A dog on his own does not go unnoticed. Harvey can hear voices shouting at him, but they're not Maggie's, and hers is the only voice that could make him turn around.

Harvey runs until a bouquet of dog scents lures him to a forest path. He finds half a sandwich and gobbles it down. Nearby he sees a small culvert with some water at the bottom, and he takes a sniff and a drink of that too. The forest is alive with sounds and smells that lead him off the gravel path and onto one that is made of bark chips. Harvey walks along this path. His curiosity takes him farther and farther away from his home.

Chapter 4

Austin

Because the old people all knew I belong to Grandpa, they were extra chatty. Some days it was hard to get anything done because of all the times I had to stop and talk with them. I complained to Grandpa about it after my first week.

"What if it was me at Brayside?" he asked. "Would you talk to me?"

"Yeah, but you're my grandpa." It was hard to imagine Grandpa ever getting old enough to live at a retirement villa.

Grandpa looked me right in the eye and said, "They're all someone's grandpa or grandma too. Treat them how you'd want me treated, okay?"

After that, I went out of my way to say hello to every old person who walked by. I listened when Miss Lin told me about the latest episode of *Dateline*. And I made sure to smile at all the right parts when I heard the story about Mrs. Gelman's grandkids for the tenth time.

That day, as I dusted the baseboards, Mrs. O'Brien asked, "How are you, Austin?" Mrs. O'Brien is one of my favorite old people at Brayside. She's got a fluffy white cloud of hair and is always trying to feed me—which is fine by me.

"Good, thanks."

"I baked blueberry muffins." She smiled. I knew there'd be a package of muffins waiting for me at the reception desk when I left. Grandpa says he's gained ten pounds off Mrs. O'Brien's baking. She had heart problems a few years ago, but you wouldn't know it. For an old person, she's got a ton of energy.

"Thanks, Mrs. O'Brien."

Mr. Santos came by next. I breathed a sigh of relief that he didn't have his daily crossword puzzle with him. But that didn't stop him from giving me a play-by-play of that day's tricky clues and how he solved them. I gave him the answer to one question the week before, and now he thinks I'm some kind of puzzle-genius. "Thirty-six Down. By which meatballs are made from stale lamb," he said, waiting for me to come up with something.

I held out my hands. "I got nothing, Mr. Santos."

"Anagram!" he said proudly. "Meatballs and stale lamb have the same letters, just mixed up. Took me almost an hour to figure it out."

"I'll have to remember that one," I said with a laugh.

Mr. Pickering's door opened. Instead of getting back to work on the baseboards, I stood up, prepared to be friendly even if he looked like he wanted to bite my head off. I wondered if Mr. Pickering was lonely because he was mean, or mean because he was lonely.

Squeezing the damp rag in my hand, I waited till he was right in front of me. "Going for dinner?" I asked. My voice came out a little squeaky.

He moved right past me like I never spoke. Lots of old people can't hear, so I tried again. "Mr. Pickering, are you going for dinner?" I said it so loud, the nurse at reception looked up.

"Where else would I be going?" His voice was gruff like always.

"It's sweet-and-sour ribs tonight," I told him. I'd seen the sign by the dining room.

Mr. Pickering looked directly at me. His eyes were watery and hidden in wrinkles. "I like those."

"Yeah, me too," I answered.

He gave a *"Harrumph"* and shuffled past me.

Lonely because he's mean, I decided, and called him an old grump under my breath.

Chapter 5

Harvey

Harvey walks through the night, snuffling through piles of wet leaves as he searches for a dry place to rest. There is a confusing tangle of scents, but nothing familiar. With his ears pricked, he catches a distant bark and follows it, arriving at the wrong side of a chain-link fence.

The forest where Harvey has been wandering backs onto a wide-open field that is known as Norman Dog Park. This early in the morning, there is only one large dog racing after a ball. Harvey can smell an array of odors and wishes he had more in his bladder so that he too could leave his mark.

Harvey sniffs along the fence, hoping for an opening. Small for a Westie, Harvey finds a space large enough for him to crawl through on his belly. The dog park does indeed reward him with all sorts of new and exciting smells. Once again, he forgets about how far he is from home. He races from tree to tree, sniffing to his heart's content. As the morning brightens, more people arrive with their dogs. It's a large park, with plenty of space for the bigger dogs. Harvey does not know to be wary of any dogs, so it comes as a surprise to him when he sees one bounding toward him, full-tilt and ready to play. Before Harvey can run, the dog has clobbered him, and Harvey is lying on his back.

Harvey scrambles, but his short legs and soft paws are no match for the power of the beast on top of him. The creature growls and snarls. Harvey twists out from under the monster as one of its paws presses down on his side. He yelps at the sharp pain on his rib and runs away as fast as he can. Thankfully, the big dog's owner is nearby and calls it off, clamping a leash onto its collar. But the man can do nothing to help Harvey, since he has his hands full with his own dog. Harvey skitters away, feeling a pang of loneliness that aches as much as his side.

Harvey is now hungry, tired, hurt, and alone. He doesn't put up a fight when he feels someone pick him up. It is another dog owner who is at the dog park with her partner. Miles and Lucy, a young couple, have seen that Harvey is in trouble. They look for his owner in the park, but of course there isn't one. They ask around, but no one has seen anyone with Harvey.

It was bad luck for Harvey to have been spotted by that brute. But it is good luck that he has been found by Lucy, since she works at a vet clinic. She and Miles discuss what to do. They wait, stroking Harvey's back and trying to calm him.

"Are you lost, Harvey?" she asks, after reading his name tag. If Harvey could answer, he'd say that he has seen enough of the world and wants to go home. The novelty of freedom has worn off.

They decide Lucy will take Harvey to the clinic where she works and use the chip in his ear to find his owner.

Lucy loads Harvey into the car. Grit from the forest has made his coat heavy. When he tries to groom himself, he gets a mouthful of dirt. It disconcerts him that the wool blanket he lies on—in fact, the whole car—is rife with another dog's odor. But he is tired, and against his instinct, Harvey lies down.

Lucy pulls up to the vet clinic and steps out of the car. At the same moment, a taxi parked ahead of her begins to pull away. Harvey has an excellent memory for smells. Every odor he has come across has been recorded and catalogued in Harvey's extensive scent memory. Some smells stand out as extraordinary because of the feelings attached to them—for example, the scent of the car that took his Maggie away.

It is the slightest whiff of the sweet and spicy taxicab that perks Harvey up.

Lucy opens the back door, prepared to lift Harvey off the seat and carry him into the clinic. Instead, she gives a surprised yelp as Harvey jumps out and darts past her. The taxi is pulling away from the curb, and with single-minded determination, Harvey races after it.

Behind him, Lucy watches in shock as the Westie takes off and then turns the corner. She runs after him, yelling, "Stop, Harvey! Come back!" Harvey does neither. The scent of the taxi is the only thing that he is paying attention to. Even as the scent fades, he keeps running, desperately hoping it will take him to his Maggie.

Panting, Lucy gives up the chase. She knows that if he was lost before, he is more lost now. Her good deed has gone hopelessly wrong. She goes back to her car and waits for a while in case the Westie returns. But he doesn't. With a heavy heart, she realizes there is nothing to do but drive back to the dog park to share the unfortunate developments with Miles. She can only hope someone else will find the dog and do a better job locating his owner than she did.

Harvey will wander aimlessly for another day, trotting down back alleys and away from the noise and exhaust fumes of downtown. He will raid garbage bags left on the street for food. He will be desperately thirsty and have to settle for a drink from a sudsy puddle outside of a restaurant.

It is late in the evening when he finds a doorstep with an overhang to protect him from the rain that has started to pelt down. He huddles against the brick wall. His skirt is muddied and tangled and covered in grit from two days of neglect. Harvey does not resemble the dog Maggie left behind except for the red harness and the silver tag dangling from his neck.

Chapter 6

Austin

"Windows," Grandpa said, and passed me a spray bottle of blue window cleaner and a rag. I knew better than to roll my eyes.

Windows actually means all the glass surfaces, and there are a lot of them. Sliding glass doors at the front of the building, mirrors in the hallway, protective glass on the tabletops, and the glass photo frames outside of every suite. The frames are for the photo collages the residents make. You can learn a lot from the collages. For instance, I never would have known Mr. Singh met the Prime Minister—the one before the one we have now—unless I'd seen the picture. And Mrs. Luzzi used to sing opera; there's a bunch of photos of her on stage in costumes.

The collage by Mr. Santos' door has photos of him and his wife by the Great Wall of China and the Taj Mahal in India. He told me he'd traveled the world and had even swum in the Dead Sea between Isreal and Jordan—although I could have done without seeing Mr. Santos in a Speedo.

"Do you miss traveling?" I asked him once.

He got a faraway look in his eye. "After my wife died, I didn't feel like it anymore. Guess it wasn't the traveling I liked so much as spending time with her. Losing people you love is the hardest part of getting old."

I guess that is true for all the people at Brayside. A lot of them are on their own now, but almost all of their collages include a wedding photo.

I was thinking about my conversation with Mr. Santos as I dusted the glass covering on Mr. Pickering's collage. Even he had a wedding picture. It was in black and white like his other photos and in it he was wearing a uniform, like from the army or something. He was smiling and actually looked happy. In another photo, he was sitting in the cockpit of a two-person plane, and a different one showed him receiving a medal. But most of the pictures were taken on a farm. And the same dog was in almost every photo. The dog was big and fluffy, with patches of white and brown and a nose like a collie. I did a double take—in one of the pictures, the dog only had three legs. Usually I didn't dawdle in front of Mr. Pickering's suite, but I had never noticed the three-legged dog before. I was so distracted by the photos, I didn't see the door open or Mr. Pickering glowering at me. I looked away, suddenly nervous.

"What are you snooping around for?"

"I'm cleaning," I said. I held up the rag as proof.

Mr. Pickering snorted. "Well, don't let me stop you."

Why are you so grumpy? I wanted to ask him. But then I looked at the collage again and remembered that he was ninety-six. I imagined how many people he'd lost. His wife. His friends. It was really sad when I thought about it.

Mr. Pickering walked past me on his way to the dining room. I went back to cleaning. But the whole time I was wiping those windows, I couldn't help wondering if I'd been wrong about Mr. Pickering. Maybe he was grumpy because he was lonely, and not the other way around.

Chapter 7

Harvey

As a dog, Harvey has no hindsight. He can't regret his decision to leave Maggie's yard or run away from Lucy. But he does grow confused as darkness falls. He can't catch the scent of home. The car headlights blind him, and unfamiliar sounds fly at him from all sides. He whimpers and spins in circles.

Eventually, he finds a spot in an alley, where the stench of garbage fills his brain. The smell is so strong he finds it a relief. Harvey's senses are on overload; his brain digs through every scent, searching for something familiar.

After only a few hours, the nearby bark of a large dog startles him awake. Harvey starts moving again.

The next day, it is midafternoon before instinct tells an exhausted and hungry Harvey to rest. He tucks himself behind a planter at the front door of Brayside Retirement Villa just before an eleven-year-old boy arrives.

Chapter 8

Austin

Brayside has an awning that stretches out to the street so the old people won't get too wet if it's raining. There's a red carpet rolled out to the street too, with Brayside written in curvy letters. If you didn't know it was a place for old people, you'd think it was a fancy hotel.

There are planters on either side of the door. Big flower arrangements filled them in summer, but now that it was fall, it was full of pumpkins and birch branches. I was so busy looking at what was in the planter that I almost missed what was lying behind it.

Two brown eyes looked up at me. I knew right away that the little guy must be lost. Mom always says not to pat strange dogs, but this one looked so pitiful, I couldn't help myself.

"Aww! Come here," I said, and held my hand out. He lifted his head, but he was trembling and looked too scared to move toward me. His coat was matted and muddy, and I wondered if he was injured.

"Come here," I tried again, patting my hand on the carpet.

Louise, one of the nurses, saw me through the glass and came outside, wrapping her sweater around her. "What'd you find?"

"A dog."

"Oh, look at the little thing," she said. "He's shaking. Bet he's hungry." She went back inside. When she came out again, she was carrying a bowl with a little bit of meat in it—probably stolen from the dining-room kitchen.

Louise put the bowl down in front of the dog. He sniffed it, and a second later it was gone.

"Told you," she said.

Louise took another piece and dropped it closer to me. The dog inched his way from behind the planter and snapped up the second piece. I put out my hand slowly and left it there so he could sniff it. I wanted him to know I was not going to hurt him.

"It's okay," I said softly. "We won't hurt you." He inched closer and Louise set the whole bowl down. The meat was gone faster than I could blink. "I wonder how long he's been lost."

"He's a sweet thing," she said. "Maybe we should bring him inside and call someone."

There was a tag hanging from his harness, which looked broken. One strap dangled and its end was frayed. I held out my hand again. This time he licked it, like he was saying thank you. I patted his head. He didn't jump away or bark, so I slid my hand to his harness and held up the tag.

"Harvey," I read.

"Harvey," Louise repeated. "Is that your name? Is it Harvey?" She said it in an excited way, and Harvey perked up.

"Think he'll let me pick him up?" I asked her. Louise shrugged.

"Only one way to find out," I muttered. I crouched down and scooped him up. He seemed so tired that he let me hold him. But I could feel him shivering.

When I brought Harvey inside, it caused a commotion. Louise started bossing everyone around—even Mary Rose, who is technically her boss. "Mary Rose," she whispered, "get a blanket. Artie, this dog needs some water." We had to whisper because Charlie was in his office. I wasn't sure dogs were allowed at Brayside. I sat down behind the reception desk and hugged Harvey against my chest to let him know he was safe.

Grandpa, up from the basement, joined the others. "What's going on?"

"Well, Phillip," Louise said, "your grandson found a dog."

"His name's Harvey," I said.

Grandpa's got a soft spot for dogs. He reached out a hand and rubbed the top of Harvey's head.

"Looks like he needs a bath."

"He should eat first," Artie said, coming back with food and water. Harvey practically leapt out of my arms when he smelled the meat in the bowl. It looked like ground beef, with a bit of gravy and potatoes mixed in.

Everyone had an opinion about what to do with Harvey. Call the vet, call the shelter, call the Humane Society, put up posters, take him home. Okay, well, taking him home was my idea; even Grandpa looked skeptical when I suggested it.

"If we take him to a shelter, he'll have to wait in a cage until they find his owner," I explained. "Isn't it better if he stays with me?"

I gave them all my best sweet-and-innocent face. Artie, Louise, and Mary Rose agreed—I should take Harvey home. But Grandpa shook his head. He knew what Mom would say if I walked in with Harvey. My sweet-and-innocent face had stopped working on her a while ago.

"Better let me do the talking for you," he said with a sigh. I grinned at Grandpa and held Harvey a little tighter. "And we'd better get Harvey cleaned up. No way is your mom going to let you bring a dirty thing like him into the apartment."

Chapter 9

Harvey

Harvey lifts his nose, trying to detect the scent of his Maggie. Peeling apart layer upon layer of smells is no easy task. But, as hard as he concentrates, his nose comes back empty.

Instinct tells him he is safe in the boy's arms, so Harvey doesn't try to jump away, even as they go down to a place that is dark and damp. Harvey's ears go down when he hears a gush of water from a tap. He knows that sound. A bath! Harvey hates baths, even though his coat is dirty and burrs are tangled in his beard.

"Don't be afraid," the boy named Austin whispers. "It's just a bath." But the stress of the last few days and the newness of this place make Harvey shiver and cower against Austin's chest. "Aw! He's scared, Grandpa!" Austin says.

The man named Phillip speaks in a soothing tone and pats Harvey's head. "Shh, shh," he whispers. "Everything's okay."

Phillip unbuckles Harvey's harness and lays it on the side of the tub. Harvey feels bare without it. "Okay, Austin, put him in real gentle." Harvey struggles to lift his paws as he's lowered into the tub. He even scratches Austin's arm in his desperation to escape. But it's no use. Warm, sudsy water swishes against his legs and belly. Austin takes handfuls of water and lets it run over Harvey's filthy coat.

Harvey snorts as water drips into his nose, surprised that today's bath isn't as horrible as the ones at Maggie's house. Austin chats to Harvey the whole time, gently pouring water from a container. Harvey can feel the knots in his fur weakening. One knot is stubborn and Austin tries to run his fingers through it, but the tug makes Harvey yelp.

"Sorry," Austin whispers.

As soon as the soap has been rinsed away with clean water, Phillip returns with a towel. The towels at Brayside are washed with special detergent to keep them soft. They sit in a fluffy pile, neatly folded on a shelf beside the dryer. He unfolds one of the towels and shakes it out. Austin lifts the dripping Harvey out of the sink and places him on the towel.

Harvey, like all dogs, hates the feeling of heavy, clinging fur. As soon as he is on the towel, he begins to shake. He shakes so violently that water spatters all over Austin and Phillip. His shaking is met with shouts and laughter, which Harvey knows is a good thing.

Harvey's coat is already springing back to life. "There now. That's better, isn't it?" Phillip says. Phillip rubs Harvey dry with the towel and checks inside his ear. "Some of them get identification tattoos in case they get lost." Harvey doesn't like having his ears yanked. He cowers. The pink flesh is numberless anyway. Phillip sighs. "Well, tomorrow you'll have to take him to a vet and see if they can find a microchip. A nice dog like this, someone must be looking for him."

Harvey feels the boy beside him tense just a little.

"You know you can't keep him," Phillip says. "He belongs to someone."

"I know." Austin picks Harvey up and holds him against his chest. Normally, Harvey would prefer to walk, but he's done so much walking lately. His legs ache and the warm bath has left him feeling sleepy.

Austin carries Harvey back to reception where there are lots of *oohs* and *ahhs* over his newly clean appearance. "Aren't you a cutie," Mary Rose says, putting her nose right up to Harvey's. Harvey likes the smell of her and the way she holds his chin in her hand. She scratches behind his ears and grins at him. "Some places have therapy dogs like him to help with the residents."

Harvey settles himself on the blanket that has been laid out for him. It is soft, much softer than the cement he slept on yesterday. He is surrounded by warmth and feels safe for the first time since he left his home. Austin's hand strokes his back. The rhythmic motion sends Harvey to sleep.

Chapter 10

Austin

I was hoping Mom's No Dogs rule would fly out the window as soon as she saw Harvey. My sweet-and-innocent face might not work anymore, but maybe Harvey's would. Mom hadn't had an easy time lately. She'd been laid off last year and had to take a job she hated. There was a frown line between her eyes that I swear got deeper every day.

"Austin!" she exclaimed when Grandpa and I walked in with Harvey. She looked at Grandpa and shook her head. "Did you agree to this?"

"He's lost, Mom."

"It's just for the one night," Grandpa added. "I'll pick him up and bring him to Brayside till Austin's done school."

Mom sighed. "We don't have a leash—"

But I held up the yellow nylon rope I used to get him here. "This works."

Mom frowned at me. She knew when she was beat. As if she could say no to a dog like Harvey, anyway.

"One night, Austin. And then he goes. It's not like we can afford a dog on top of everything else."

"One night," I agreed.

I heard her and Grandpa talk in low voices while I followed Harvey around on his inspection of our apartment. It's small, but it was probably filled with new smells. "Come on, Harvey," I said and went to my room. I dumped the clothes out of my dresser drawer and lined it with a towel I had grabbed from the bathroom. I wanted him to try out his new bed, but he was still too busy checking out his new home.

Mom said one night only. But what if his owners didn't want him anymore? What if they offered to let me keep him? I bet Mom wouldn't say no to that. How could she?

The next day at school, all I could think about was Harvey. The night before, instead of sleeping in the drawer, he'd jumped onto my bed and curled up on my feet. Thinking about it made me smile. I caught Mom patting him before she left for work.

I knew I'd promised Mom he'd only be with us for one night. But I hated the thought of leaving Harvey at a shelter.

If I'd had a dog like Harvey, I'd never let him run away, that was for sure. I wondered what kind of an owner couldn't look after their dog. Maybe Harvey ran away *for a reason*. Or maybe his owner didn't want him anymore—in that case, there'd be no point looking for him.

What if his owner hurt Harvey? I got a twist in my gut thinking about it. There was no way I could send Harvey back to a person who didn't take good care of him—that made the decision for me.

I wasn't going to take him to the animal shelter. I'd say I went but that they couldn't find the owner and asked me to keep him. Those shelters are always overcrowded with abandoned pets, so I was sure that Mom would believe me.

But then I had another thought. What if Harvey was my dog and I lost him? I'd want whoever found him to help get him back to me. Saying I'd gone to the shelter and then keeping him was like stealing—*and* I'd be lying to Grandpa and Mom. I wrestled the thoughts back and forth all day, hoping that by the time I got to Brayside after school, I'd know what to do.

Chapter 11

Harvey

Harvey arrives at Brayside with Phillip to find a new collar, leash, and a proper dog bed, dug out of Artie's basement. They belonged to a long-gone pet, and Harvey smells her odor as soon as he settles into her bed, which has been tucked under the reception desk.

Harvey doesn't spend much time there. He has too much work to do. The whole main floor must be inspected and sniffed. There is a couch in front of the window in the entrance, and Harvey is just tall enough to stretch his front paws and see over the back of it. From this location, he can scout the sidewalk for intruders. The sliding-glass doors make a curious *shushing* noise that draws him to them every time they open and close.

Of course the old people all want to see Harvey. Mary Rose finds a tennis ball and they play a game of roll-the-ball in the games room. The laughter of the old people is low and soft, like a gentle breeze. Harvey is so busy, he almost forgets his Maggie. But when he retreats to his bed under the reception desk for a rest, it's her scent he longs for.

He has just dozed off when he hears his name. "Hey, Harvey!" A leash dangles in front of him and the boy says the magic word: "Walk."

The leash is clipped onto his collar. Harvey tugs, eager to get outside. His nose is alert, ready for the onslaught of new odors. "Whoa, Harvey." Austin laughs. The leash goes slack, so Harvey knows he has permission to run.

Austin lets Harvey run for blocks, stopping at the spots where the air gets thick with exhaust and metal and hot rubber. They go all the way to a spot where Harvey's nose twitches with new smells—layers and layers of them! He sprinkles where he can to let whoever else might show up know he's been there. Harvey zips from tree to tree and every fire hydrant in between. Even the corners of buildings are filled with the scents of other dogs. Harvey is so preoccupied with the layers of scents that he doesn't notice the change in Austin.

"Harvey," Austin says, pulling him away from a tuft of grass. His voice is strained, and Harvey pricks his ears to figure out why. There are animals inside the building. Harvey can hear their barks bounce off the windows. As soon as the door is opened, the barking becomes clearer. The other dogs are warning him.

"Out!"

"Don't come closer!"

"Danger!"

Harvey's tail goes up and he freezes. He won't go one step closer. Harvey looks up at Austin and their eyes lock.

"I can't do it," Austin mumbles. "Come on, Harvey. Let's go home."

Chapter 12

The first words out of Grandpa's mouth when he saw me with Harvey were: "I thought you were going to the shelter. That's what I told Charlie."

I let go of Harvey's leash, and he ran to greet Grandpa, his tail wagging a hundred miles an hour.

"I did. They said they were full." The lie came off my tongue so easily. "They asked if I could keep him till there's space. They'll call Brayside if they find his owner."

Grandpa frowned for a moment, then bent down to pat Harvey's head. "Don't worry, little guy. We'll find your home."

He is *home*, I wanted to say.

While Harvey slept, worn out from our run, Grandpa asked me to dust the baseboards—again. I wanted to tell him I'd just dusted them last week, and that old people weren't *that* dirty. Plus, even if the baseboards were covered in an inch of dust, none of the old people could bend down far enough to see them. But I kept my lips zipped. I was still on probation for the fireworks, and I had Harvey to think about now. I didn't want to give Grandpa or Mom any reason to take him away.

I crabwalked along the floor with my spray bottle and cloth, but I didn't get very far before my legs ached and I had to stand up. I could hear someone walking toward me. It was a shuffle more than a walk. The slipper bottoms sounded like sandpaper against the floor.

Behind me, the shuffling stopped. I waited, expecting it to start again, and when it didn't, I turned around. Mr. Pickering was standing in the middle of the hallway looking confused. Being around old people so much, I've seen it happen before. If it were anyone else, I'd offer to help, but I was worried Mr. Pickering would bite my head off.

Finally, he spoke. "Which way's my room?" It was more of a bark than a question.

I couldn't ignore him, so I stood up and pointed down the hallway. He took a few steps, but it was slow going. He looked a little wobbly too.

"Want to take my arm?" I asked, holding it out. I thought, *No way is he going to say yes*—but he did. I took small steps so he could keep up, and we walk-shuffled down the hall to his room.

"Mrs. O'Brien's been baking. Smells like cinnamon buns," I said, because it felt awkward to be so close and not talk.

He paused and took a quick breath. "Apple crisp."

I glanced at Mr. Pickering out of the corner of my eye. "Do you like apple crisp?"

"Rather have pie."

Before I could stop it, a smile lifted one side of my mouth. "Yeah. Me too."

"You're Phillip's grandson?" he croaked when we reached his door.

"Yes, sir." I'd never in my life called anyone "sir" before, but Mr. Pickering was the type of person who looked like he expected it.

"Tell your grandfather I have a burned-out lightbulb."

"Yes, sir," I said again, and opened the door to his apartment for him.

At the other end of the hallway, Harvey had woken up from his nap. He looked like the dog version of a mad scientist; one side of his face had been crushed against his pillow, and his hair stuck straight up. Halfway down the hall, he stopped to shake out his coat. Then he picked up the pace, and in a second, he was at my side.

Mr. Pickering looked down at Harvey and said, "What's that dog doing here?"

Explaining the story would have taken too long, so I said, "Harvey's mine." In case Mr. Pickering was nervous about dogs, I added, "He's really friendly."

As if to prove my point, Harvey moved to Mr. Pickering and took a good, long sniff of his leather slippers. Then he reached his front paws up Mr. Pickering's legs as if he was stretching to get closer. Mr. Pickering reached out a gnarled old-man hand and patted Harvey on the head.

"You're a good dog," he said and chuckled.

I stared at Mr. Pickering as if I weren't seeing things right. It only lasted for a second, though, before his face went back to its usual frown.

"Don't forget about the light. It's been burned out for two days."

"Yes, sir," I mumbled as Mr. Pickering went into his suite and shut the door.

I found Grandpa coming out of his office, carrying a plunger. "Mr. Pickering needs a lightbulb changed," I told him.

"You can handle that," he said. "Unless you'd rather un-clog a toilet." I shook my head and grabbed a lightbulb from the supply closet. Harvey was at my heels the whole time, curious to see what I was doing and sniffing at all the new spaces.

"We can do this, Harvey," I said, mostly to pump myself up.

It helped to have Harvey with me, like my canine support crew, as I knocked on Mr. Pickering's door.

I knew better than to knock a second time. Old people move like they're in slow motion. One thing about coming to Brayside so often is that I've learned to be patient. They really are going as fast as they can.

While I was waiting, I took another look at Mr. Pickering's photo collage. There was a photo of a boy about my age with a big grin on his face—I assumed that was Mr. Pickering, although it was hard to tell. The dog was in that photo too, and a girl. Her hair was cut short and uneven, like she did it herself. She was wearing a grubby dress. Just looking at her, I could tell she was one of those kids who'd rather be digging for worms than standing still for a photo. Behind them was a house and a field, and an old farm truck was parked in the driveway. There was a date stamped on the bottom: 1933.

When the door finally opened, I held the lightbulb up so Mr. Pickering could see it. "Grandpa was busy, so he sent me."

Mr. Pickering grunted and opened the door wider. "It's that lamp, right there." He pointed to one on the table by a recliner. Even though cleaners came once a week, Mr. Pickering's room had a musty, old-man smell. He was wearing a sweater despite the room being hot and stuffy. There were all kinds of books on the shelves, and a TV—the old kind, not a flat-screen. It was set to the weather channel, which was kind of funny, since I'd never seen him go outside.

A knitted blanket was draped over a couch. A stack of newspapers sat on the counter.

I felt him watching me as I unscrewed the little brass cap and lifted off the shade so I could replace the bulb.

"You're a good boy," Mr. Pickering said.

I was about to say thanks, but when I turned around I could see that he was talking to Harvey. I almost laughed out loud. Harvey's tail was wagging like a windshield wiper as Mr. Pickering scratched under his chin.

It only took a minute to screw the new bulb in place and put the shade back on. "All done." I turned on the light to prove it.

Mr. Pickering gave Harvey a pat on the head and shuffled over to his recliner. He sat down heavily.

"I had a dog. His name was General."

I froze right where I was in case any sudden movement would stop him talking. "Is that the dog in the picture?"

"Eh?" Mr. Pickering turned to me as if he'd forgotten I was there.

"Outside your door. It looked like you were on a farm. There was a three-legged dog."

Mr. Pickering looked so confused that I wished I hadn't said anything. I considered saying *Never mind* and making a quick getaway. Or I could bring him the photo collage. I knew what Grandpa would want me to do, so I went into the hallway and took the collage off the wall.

"See, that dog." I pointed to the photo I was looking at before. "He's only got three legs."

Lots of old people tremble. Everything about them is shaky—how they walk, their hands, even some of their mouths can't seem to stay still. Mr. Pickering was no different. His hand fluttered to the frame as he pulled it closer.

"That's him," he said. "Haven't thought about that dog in a long time." He looked at me with eyes half buried under folds of skin, and frowned.

"How'd he lose his leg?"

"How should I know?" Mr. Pickering pushed the photo frame back at me, annoyed.

I took a step back and wished I hadn't asked. I turned to go, with Harvey at my heels.

"Leave it," Mr. Pickering barked. He meant the photo frame. I put it on the table beside his recliner and shut the door after me.

As soon as we were in the hallway, I looked down at Harvey. He might be the dog, but Mr. Pickering was the one with the bite.

Chapter 13

Maggie

Across town and a few days later, a taxi pulls into the drive-way of Maggie's house. It is Sunday night, and Maggie's family has returned from their weeklong holiday, exhausted after a long day of travel.

Maggie's parents have spent the last five days hiding the truth about Harvey's disappearance from their daughter. That first day, Olivia had searched desperately for hours before she called with her gut-wrenching confession.

Maggie's parents had discussed the matter at length, but in the end decided that Olivia was doing everything she could to find the little dog. Cutting the family holiday short so they could find Harvey didn't make sense. As worrisome as it was, they were sure Harvey would be found, but so far Olivia's search has been fruitless.

Olivia, too ashamed to face them, isn't at Maggie's house when the family arrives—which is just as well. The twins have fallen asleep in the taxi, and it is quite an ordeal to carry them and the luggage inside. Maggie is conscripted to be the door-holder, and it takes Maggie's father three trips to get everything. After the taxi has pulled out of the driveway, it is a few minutes before Maggie wonders why Harvey hasn't come to the door to greet her.

"Harvey," she calls quietly.

Her mother closes the twins' bedroom door after putting them in their beds. From the top of the stairs, she says, "Harvey's not here, honey."

"Where is he?"

It is two in the morning, and Maggie's mother doesn't have the emotional energy to tell the truth and deal with the fall-out. So she lies. It is a lie that will buy her some time and a good night's sleep. Tomorrow, she will tell Maggie the truth and do everything she can to make sure Harvey is found. But for right now, a lie is all she has the energy for.

"Olivia took him to her house."

"Why?"

Maggie's mother hesitates. "So we could sleep in tomorrow."

Maggie sighs with disappointment but is too tired to argue. *It's just one more night*, she thinks to herself. *And then I'll have Harvey back.*

Chapter 14

Austin

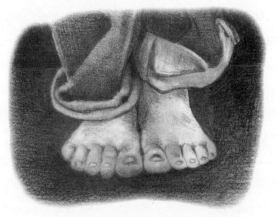

Lucky for me, Charlie is cheap. As soon as he found out how much it would cost to have a real therapy dog, he was happy to let Harvey hang out for free. I wasn't sure who let him think Harvey was trained, but I wasn't complaining. Neither was Harvey.

Harvey jumped up from his bed behind the reception desk when I arrived at Brayside on Monday. After spending all weekend together, I missed him when I was at school. "How was he?" I asked Artie, who was stationed at the reception desk.

"Took him out a couple of hours ago. He's probably due to go out again. Any luck finding his owner?"

"No luck," I said and hoped he wouldn't notice the guilty flush that spread up my neck.

"By the way," Artie said, "Mr. Singh bought an electric scooter. He takes the corners a little fast, so be careful. He almost mowed down Mr. and Mrs. Kowalski this morning."

"The Cobra GT4? He's been talking about that thing for weeks!" With low-profile tires, an LED headlight, and a swivel captain seat, even I was a little excited to see it in action. Maybe he'd let me take a spin on it.

"It goes ten miles an hour, which doesn't sound fast till you see him take off down the hallway. I've been keeping Harvey close."

"Thanks," I said. I didn't want to think about what would happen if Harvey got tangled up under the Cobra's wheels. Brayside roadkill.

"Also, Mr. Santos left a message for you." Artie pulled a yellow sticky note off the reception desk. "Nine Across. Video game icon, six letters. First letter: *A*."

"Avatar," I said, figuring Artie probably knew the answer too. I took the sticky note and headed toward Mr. Santos' door.

Monday was usually the day Grandpa made me shine the silverware—the world's most boring task. I was in no rush to do that, so after I delivered the answer for Nine Across to Mr. Santos, I took Harvey to the courtyard. Some of the old people in the games room watched through the window as I tossed the ball. He raced after it in a white blur of fur. I felt a pinch in my heart as I thought about what would have happened if I had let the shelter check his microchip. They'd have called his owners and I would have lost him already.

When we came inside, Harvey sniffed at Mr. Pickering's door.

"Come on, Harvey," I said and slapped my thigh. But he ignored me and sat down. "Really?" I said, exasperated. "Him? Of all the people at Brayside, he's the one you want to visit?"

To answer my question, Harvey lifted a paw and scratched the door. I thought about the pile of silverware and the smelly polishing cream, and how much I hated that chore. Grandpa would be happy if he found out I'd been hanging with Mr. Pickering, but after my last visit, I was worried he'd bite my head off again. I stared at the door, trying to decide. Polishing silverware versus cranky old man. It was a tough choice. The hook where the photo collage hung was still empty. If something happened to it, it would be my fault. I knocked on the door, half-hoping he wouldn't answer.

He opened the door a crack and peered out at me.

"Hi, Mr. Pickering."

"Who are you?"

"Austin, Phillip's grandson. Remember? I hang out here after school." I looked down at Harvey. "And this is Harvey."

"Since when are dogs allowed at hotels?"

I wasn't expecting that. "Well, uh, this isn't a hotel. It's Brayside. Harvey's a therapy dog," I said quickly, starting to believe it myself.

"Did my wife call you?"

"Your wife? Ah, no." I realized this was a bad idea. "We'll come back later," I said quickly and turned to go.

He opened the door wider. "I know you," he said, and looked down at Harvey. "That's your dog."

"Yeah," I answered, relieved.

"Do you want to come in?" He held the door open and Harvey trotted in like it had been his home forever. Mr. Pickering shuffled back to his recliner. Harvey put his front paws up on the seat and jumped up. *Harvey's got some guts*, I thought as he cuddled up against Mr. Pickering's leg.

Mr. Pickering looked as surprised as I was. He frowned at Harvey like he wasn't sure if he should shoo him away or just settle in and enjoy the company.

I was still standing by the door, but it looked like we were staying for a while, so I moved in and perched on the edge of the couch. I was relieved to see the photo collage lying on the table beside a cup of tea. There was an awkward silence as Mr. Pickering patted Harvey.

"Want me to hang the photo frame back up?" I asked.

"I've been looking at it. Remembering." He got a wistful look on his face, and for a second the grumpy Mr. Pickering was replaced with someone else.

I wanted to know more about when he flew planes and got the medals, but it was the photo of him with the girl and the three-legged dog that I was most curious about.

"Is that your sister?" I asked, pointing to the picture of the kids.

Mr. Pickering cleared his throat. I half expected him to tell me to get lost, like he did the last time. "Her name was Bertie. She wasn't my sister; she was my friend. And tougher than most boys her age, including me."

"She looked like it," I agreed.

"We got into our share of trouble—me, her, and General." There wasn't much padding on the arm of the couch and the wooden frame dug into my butt, but I didn't dare move, worried that Mr. Pickering would stop talking.

"How'd you meet her?" I asked.

His eyebrows pulled together as he thought about it. "Must have been the summer of '33, because the droughts hadn't started yet. Or not so we were aware of them." Harvey sighed, his chin resting on his paws, and I wondered if he could look more comfortable. "It was by the bridge at Shell Creek. She'd just moved to town. Her pa was a thresher, gone for harvest. She lived in a shack not far from the creek."

Mr. Pickering rested his head against the back of the chair. I thought he was done talking, and I was about to stand up and wake Harvey when he said, "That summer, me, my twin brothers, Millard and Nigel—holy terrors that they were—and little Eugene Aikins from down the road walked to our swimming spot on the Shell Creek almost every day. We'd strip down to our skivvies, or sometimes nothing at all, and spend a couple of hours playing in the water. I remember," he said, turning his head my way, "there was a patch of wild strawberries along the shore, and we'd pick them when they were in season. Sometimes, we'd make a fishing pole with a strip of willow and dangle a minnow we caught or a worm we dug up in Ma's garden. Wasn't much to catch in Shell Creek, but we tried anyhow.

"General would come along with us. He still had four legs back then. I don't think I went anywhere without General. I had just turned ten in June, but I looked younger. I was wiry and small, and jealous of my brothers. They were stocky and no one pushed them around."

I was pretty scrawny too compared to some of the kids at school, so I knew how he felt.

"What was I telling you?" Mr. Pickering asked, turning to me.

"About how you met Bertie," I reminded him. "You were swimming at Shell Creek. Summer of—"

"Thirty-three. Right. General went to sniffing in the bush while the twins and Eugene speared crayfish. I sat on a rock that we named Big Yellow. It had streaks of ochre running through it. Biggest boulder anywhere around. Perfect for jumping into the water.

"All of a sudden, there was a commotion in the bush, and General backed out, barking. I thought maybe he'd found a coyote; there were always a few hanging around the farm, hoping to steal some of Ma's chickens.

"Usually, General chased the coyote away, but with all the barking, I wondered if it was something worse, like a pack of wild dogs stalking us. Let me tell you, my heart was pounding when I stood up on the rock to get a look. A few kids and a farm dog were no match for hungry wild dogs.

"That was when I heard her. 'Get your mangy mutt outta here!' a voice yelled.

"The twins and Eugene scrambled to the bank.

"'Who's there?' I yelled back, deepening my voice so I sounded older.

"'None of your dang business! That dog gone yet?' From the shadows of the bush, I could see a skinny white thing.

"'His name's General, and he's right beside me.' Next thing I knew, this girl stepped out of the forest. Her name was Bertie Gamache. She was skinny as a rail and wearing just her skivvies too. Freckles covered her skin and she had two long braids of red hair. She glared at all of us, her chin stuck out and eyes narrowed.

"'You all make a lot of noise. I thought there was twenty of you, not just four.'

"'Who are you?' Eugene asked. I remember he stabbed his stick into the ground like he was staking a claim.

"'Bertie. Just moved here.'

"'What're you doing in the bush?' I asked, though I could see she was shivering and her hair was damp.

"'I *was* swimming, and then you lot came around like a bunch of hooligans. I was trying to get changed when your attack dog came after me.'

"Well." Mr. Pickering blew out a puff of air. "General was no attack dog. Not unless he had to be, but I didn't want to let on to the girl. I didn't want to be unfriendly to her either, 'specially since she'd just moved here. So I went about with the introductions. 'I'm Walter and these are my brothers, Nigel and Millard. And our friend Eugene.' I gave her the once-over. 'Where'd you move to?' Best I knew, there weren't any vacant farms around, unless she'd been hired on by someone—but no one had money for that. Even at ten, I knew things were getting lean for people living where we did."

Mr. Pickering turned to me. "You know anything about the Dirty Thirties?" he asked me. "Or the Dust Bowl?"

I shook my head.

He grunted like he wasn't surprised. "Don't know what they're teaching you in school," he muttered. "See, farmers can't make a living if the price of wheat goes down. Well, Number One Northern was what everyone was growing back then, and it fell below forty cents a bushel in 1932. I remember, because it was on everyone's tongues—the price of wheat and the weather."

He looked at me like this was important and I better be paying attention, which I was.

"We'd had two bad summers in a row. Hot, dry winds blew across the fields, carrying topsoil away. The sun had scorched that sprouting wheat and shriveled it. We didn't look out on fields of green anymore as we rode into town. Instead, we saw only long stretches of barren land.

"It was getting hard enough that some families had already left, so I wasn't sure what Bertie's family had been thinking coming to Wilcox. 'Just up that way, along the creek,' she said, pointing vaguely in a direction away from town.

"The only thing up that way was an abandoned shack that fur traders had used back in the day. It was half fallen-down and stunk like rotten meat. All us kids were afraid of it and said it was haunted. We used to dare each other to stand inside and count the seconds before we burst out, terrified.

"'You mean the trappers' shack?' Eugene asked. No mistaking his surprise, not with the way he wrinkled up his face.

"'Got a roof, don't it? And four walls.' Her shoulders straightened and she puffed her scrawny chest out, daring us to say anything else. Water dripped off her dark orange braids and slid down her shivering shoulders. I figured anyone who could look that fierce half-naked and cold was no one to mess with, no matter how scrawny she looked. So I kept my trap shut.

"'You coming swimming, or what?' Millard called to her. Bertie glanced at all of us, shrugged her shoulders, and took a running leap into the water, curling her legs to her chest and landing with a gigantic splash. The twins and Eugene joined in, and in seconds they had a water fight going. Bertie went after my brothers like a banshee. It took me a minute longer to decide I wasn't playing the role of big brother today, and then I jumped off Big Yellow to join them."

I couldn't tell if Mr. Pickering was done or just taking a break. I waited a minute, hoping he'd tell me more. Then I heard a snore. I guessed he was worn out from talking so long.

I went to the door, expecting Harvey to follow me, but he didn't budge. *"Harvey,"* I whispered. "Come *here.*" I had to call him two more times before he jumped off the recliner and followed me into the hallway. I shut the door quietly behind me.

Grandpa was at the reception desk, chatting to Mary Rose. "Where were you?" he asked, looking at his watch. It was almost quitting time.

"With Mr. Pickering," I said. The two of them exchanged a look as if they didn't believe me. "You were right. He's got some good stories about when he was a kid."

A slow smile spread across Grandpa's face. "So, you cracked the shell of that old nut, eh?"

Beside him, Mary Rose snorted. I grinned too, but I knew it was more Harvey than me that got Mr. Pickering talking.

Chapter 15

Harvey

When Harvey sits beside Mr. Pickering, he drifts off into a place of contentment. It is different than his sleeps at Austin's house. The boy moves a lot, even in his sleep. Harvey is often woken up by an unexpected leg spasm that forces him to circle till he finds a new spot. But this man beside him now is still. Harvey likes the deep, musky smell of the room, soothing his overworked senses. There is a lot of coming and going at Brayside, but Harvey has learned that he doesn't have to alert anyone. In such a busy place, it is better to rest behind the desk until Austin reappears, so that is what he does.

Austin is kind to him. He feeds him and takes him out and comforts him. Harvey repays the care with loyalty. He will follow Austin and listen to his commands because he has been trained this way. But in his heart, Harvey wishes he could stay on the recliner beside Mr. Pickering.

Chapter 16

Austin

On Tuesday, I stood outside Mr. Pickering's door, debating whether or not to knock again. Harvey wanted me to. His tail was sticking straight up, his nose as close to the door as possible without going through it.

What if Monday was a fluke?

But what if it wasn't?

What if all Mr. Pickering needed was someone to listen to his stories, just like Grandpa thought? So, I took a deep breath and rapped my knuckles on the door.

I heard the creak of the recliner and a few muttered curse words on the other side of the door.

The door opened a crack. "You again," he said.

"I—uh…"

"Spit it out."

"Lightbulbs. I wanted to make sure you didn't have any more burned out." It was a lame excuse, and I wouldn't have been surprised if he shut the door in my face. But he didn't. He opened it a little wider and Harvey scooted inside.

Mr. Pickering watched Harvey jump onto the recliner. He didn't snarl that dogs weren't allowed at Brayside, or scold me for not being able to control Harvey. Instead, he shook his head like it was a losing battle.

"What's his name?" Mr. Pickering asked. He walked back to the recliner, so I guessed that it was okay if I followed him inside the apartment.

"Harvey."

He grunted. "You gave a dog a man's name." I couldn't tell if that was a good thing or a bad thing.

"It was the name he came with," I said. "What about General? Who named him?"

"All our dogs were named General."

"Which one was with you when you met Bertie?"

He nudged Harvey aside so he could sit down and then looked at me, confused. "Did I tell you about that?"

I'm used to old people being a little forgetful. Like Mrs. Gelman with the stories about her grandkids. Mr. Singh had already showed me the features of his Cobra GT4 three times. "Yeah, yesterday. It was a good story."

"Did I tell you about the day we walked to Hackett's?"

"Nope."

Mr. Pickering relaxed into his chair and rested his head against the back. His hand fell on Harvey's back and it stayed there, as if it were totally normal for Harvey to be sitting beside him.

"General came with me everywhere back then. So did Bertie, come to think of it. This one day, we were walking to Hackett's, the only store in town. We'd managed to escape Millard and Nigel for an afternoon. My older sister Amy watched the twins because Ma thought Wilcox was too far for the boys. They begged and pleaded, but thankfully Ma stayed firm and offered to belt them if they kept complaining.

"See, Ma wasn't one for messing around. She had a farm to look after, five children, and a husband who left her in the winter to work in the bush. Soon as the wheat was harvested and taken to the grain elevator, my pa would head off to work for the MacDonald Lumber Company. His days at home with us were numbered. Not that he was home much anyway. This time of year, he was out in the field, overseeing the harvest. I should have been there too, but Ma needed groceries to feed the field hands and she didn't have time to go, so the job fell to me and Bertie.

"First time Bertie came calling around the house, Ma looked at her through the window. 'That child's poor as dirt,' she muttered. She put some biscuits in a kerchief and handed them to me. We didn't have much either, with seven of us to feed, but Ma was always one for showing kindness. 'Give these to that girl.'

"I took them, and snuck one for myself as I walked out to greet Bertie. We'd been playing together all summer. The twins were crazy about her; she was as wild as they were. Sometimes I tried to be the voice of reason, but most of the time, it was easier to just go along with their antics. Our latest activity was shooting with our slingshots."

Mr. Pickering paused and looked at me. "You know how to make a slingshot?" I shook my head.

"Well, I'll tell you. I'd find a branch with a V in it, peel the bark off, and let the wood dry out. Then I'd take a sealer ring from Ma's canning supplies and use a square piece of cloth for the pouch, where I could put a rock. I made some for my brothers and Bertie, and we spent plenty of time shooting at squirrels, birds, rabbits, and gophers. Especially gophers, since those danged things drove us crazy. They dug holes all over the field and ruined our crop. My pa promised us a penny for every gopher tail we brought him. We kept our slingshots and a few rocks in our pockets at all times. We thought of ourselves as a gang, like the outlaws who had pistols in their holsters.

"So this one day, Bertie and I were walking to town. I got Ma's list crinkling in the pocket of my pants. The deerflies bit at my ankles, since my pants were too short. The walk to town was dry and dusty. I wished I could have hitched Victor to the wagon and drove him to town instead, since I was old enough. But Pa needed the horse out on the field.

"Bertie kicked a rock my way and I returned it. We passed the time in silence like that, the rock bouncing back and forth between us. I had still never been to Bertie's house, though I knew where it was. Ma's comment about Bertie being 'poor as dirt' had got me thinking. I only ever saw her in the same ragged dress, which hit well above her knees. I could see the scrapes and bruises that covered her legs. Her leather shoes had holes in them. She was clean, though. Her skin was scrubbed and her hair was always brushed and braided.

"My brothers and I avoided our weekly bath, staying outside till Ma gave up on us and used the bath water for laundry instead. We spent most of the summer in the creek anyway, but I dreaded winter when escaping the bath wasn't so easy. My skin itched from November to March with the lye soap Ma made us wash with.

"'What does your ma do?'" I asked Bertie. "'When your pa's gone threshing?'

"'Don't know,' came her reply.

"'What do you mean?'

"Bertie shrugged. 'Don't have one.'

"'Where'd she go?'

"'Died when I was a baby.'

"'Who does all the cooking and washing?' The answer came to me even as the question left my lips.

"'I do.' We fell back to silence till Bertie said, 'Who's that?' On the road ahead were two boys, one bigger than the other. They'd found a wheel with two broken spokes. They were rolling it between them. Even from this far away, I could hear a nasty laugh I recognized, and stopped walking.

"'Let's duck into the bushes and take a different way into town,' I said. Bertie looked at me like I was crazy. Thickets of gnarled shrubs lined each side of the road. I wanted to believe they'd be thick enough to conceal us from him.

"'There is no different way. We're almost there.'

"'That's Herbie Caldwell,' I said, as if that would explain things. 'The other one is Davey Elliot.'

"By now, the boys had spotted us and were rolling the wheel in our direction, chasing it with a stick. Bertie bent down and picked up the rock we'd been kicking between us and put it in the pocket of her dress. 'Come on,' she said. I had no choice but to follow her.

"You see, Herbie had never liked me and I wasn't sure why. I was scrawny and no match for him physically, but every chance he got, he would pick on me. Sometimes, Amy ran to get the teacher at recess when the beatings got especially bad, but most of the time, he could pin me against a wall behind the school and get in a good punch to the gut before anyone noticed.

"I hadn't seen Herbie all summer, and my heart beat hard as we walked toward him and Davey. Now that Davey had moved to town, the two of them were thick as thieves. Davey was the same age as the twins and didn't used to be so bad. But as we got close, I could see the same sneer on Davey's face as on Herbie's.

"'Walt!' Herbie cackled. 'Got yerself a girlfriend?'

"I ignored Herbie, intending to plough through the boys and continue our walk to town. Bertie had other ideas.

"'I'm Bertie.' She stopped and stared him right in the eye.

"Herbie narrowed his eyes at her. 'Who says I wanted to know?'

"Bertie shrugged, although she didn't drop her gaze. But she was so slight compared to Herbie's bulk. The two boys moved to the center of the path, blocking our way. If I'd been by myself, I'd have turned tail and run. I might not have been strong, but at least I could outrun Herbie, and probably Davey too. General had gone into the bush, but I figured soon as he heard our voices, he'd come bounding out to find us. Bertie continued walking as if the boys weren't there. Balling up my fists, I went with her, steeling myself for a beating.

"'Where do you think you're going?' Herbie said.

"Bertie looked right at Herbie. 'To Hackett's. Want to come?'

"I'd never wanted to belt Bertie before, but at that moment I could have socked her.

"'We don't go around with wimps.'

"'Me neither.' She took a step to the right to get past Herbie. He moved to block her. She went the other way and so did he. Watching him mess with her was like taunting a wild cat.

"Her eyes narrowed. 'You better move out of the way, if you know what's good for you.'

"This threat sent Herbie into a fit of laughter. 'Oh, yeah? You and what army? Look at Walt. He's so scared of me, he's gonna wet his pants.'

"'He feels sorry for you, you big lug. You're dumb as a post and got no hope for nothing 'round here. Not like Walter. He's goin' places, ain't you?' She paused to look at me—but not long enough to let me get a word in. 'Bet your folks ain't got two nickels to rub together right now. And here you are picking a fight with us who never even bothered you. Ain't you got anything better to do?' Bertie's rapid-fire mouth was too much for Herbie. Whatever she thought she'd accomplish by yakking his ear off, it didn't work. I saw his fists go up and he ran at me like a railway car.

"His punch got me in the shoulder, and I hit the ground with a thud, gasping for breath. Then he was on top of me, going for softer parts, aiming for my kidneys and stomach. Davey, that little weasel, yelled, 'Yeah! Get him!' from the sidelines. I closed my eyes, trying to protect myself and push him off at the same time. Let me tell you, I was hurting something bad.

"All of a sudden, I heard a crack, which I thought came from some part of me. But then Herbie's weight fell off me. He writhed on the ground and squealed in pain. I crawled away and staggered to my feet. Bertie stood ready, slingshot loaded. She glared at Davey, daring him to do anything about it.

"'Pick on someone your own size,' she spat at Herbie. She must have hit him in the ribs, because he was holding his side and wailing. Davey ran to his friend, crouching over him.

"I whistled for General, and he came bounding out of the woods. 'Lotta good you are.' I shook my head at him. My insides felt like they were gonna split in two, but I forced myself to keep pace with Bertie as she turned toward town. She didn't run but walked real quick, elbows flying out on either side of her, braids bouncing off her shoulders. We didn't stop till we reached the front steps of Hackett's.

"'That Herbie's something else,' Bertie said as droplets of sweat dripped down her temples.

"I was glad the walk had left me red-faced so she couldn't see the blush that rose up my neck at the thought of her saving my hide back there.

"When we went inside the store, I gave Mr. Hackett the list Ma had written out for him.

"'And two strings of licorice and some of those lemon drops, please.'

Mr. Hackett had a face so red and shiny it looked like it wanted to explode. He and his wife lived in the back of the store and had no children. In the winter when Pa was working in the bush, he'd welcome Ma to the store with some cake and tea.

"'You brought some muscle to help you with all this,' he said jokingly as he looked over at Bertie. Little did he know how right he was.

"Bertie grinned and stuffed the candy in her pocket.

"'Thanks, Mr. Hackett,' I said, and swung the bag of flour over my shoulder. Pa could carry 100 pounds home from the store, but Ma had taken pity on me and only ordered twenty. Even that much would make my knees tremble by the time I got home. Bertie carried another bag with cornstarch and salt. At least sucking on a lemon drop helped ease the weight some. The bell on the door jingled as we made our way back out into the heat of the day.

"'Thanks for the candy. My gran used to buy me those.'

"'You got a gran?' I wondered why she didn't live with her, instead of in the shack with her pa.

"'Yeah. She's dead now.'

"'That why you moved here?' I asked as we walked back down the dirt road. I kept an eye out for Herbie, but he was nowhere to be seen. For all his big talk, he was a coward when the beating went the other way.

"'She couldn't take care of me when she got sick. Pa had to come back and get me. She died after I left.'

"'My granddad died too. It's his farm we're on. Well, he bought it and dug the pond. Then Pa bought more land. Granddad used to live with us.'

"Memories of my granddad were hazy by then, but I remembered sitting on his knee when I was little, and his pipe smoke filling the house.

"'Bet you were glad to be back with your pa,' I said, trying to find some silver lining. Bertie just looked at me, and the curtain of toughness fell away.

"For a second, I thought she might cry. Her nostrils flared a little as she held that emotion in and jutted out her chin. 'Not really.'

"'Why not?'

"Her eyes strayed to a bruise on her arm. I didn't say anything else. I'd thought all the bruises on her were from climbing trees and playing kickball with me and the twins. Shows you how much I knew about life back then. Couldn't imagine a father doing that to his girl.

"'That ain't right,' I said finally.

"Bertie didn't say anything back, just stared at the ground. The sack of flour on my skinny back made it hard to do anything but concentrate on keeping one foot in front of the other.

"We were almost at the house when Bertie set down her bag of groceries. 'It's not his fault, you know. He never asked to have me with him. He's doing the best he can.' I gave her a solemn nod. She hesitated. By now, the bag of flour felt like it was breaking my bones. But I could tell whatever she had to say was important, so I tried my best to wait patiently, sweat trickling down my back.

"'You're the best friend I ever had,' she blurted.

"I stood stock-still while Bertie tore off away from the house, her braids and the skirt of her dress flying behind her.

"'It's about time!' Ma called from inside. All the windows were open. I lugged the flour the last few yards to the front porch and set it down with a relieved thud. 'Where's Bertie going?'

"'Home, I guess.'

"'Made her some lunch.'

"'She'll be back.'

"And of course she was." Mr. Pickering paused. "You know, we never mentioned her declaration of friendship again, or what her pa was doing to her; but it sat between us like an anchor. No matter how bad the winds were that swept across the prairie or how dark the dust clouds were that gathered on the horizon, we knew we had each other."

When Mr. Pickering was done speaking, he looked exhausted. I never knew an old person could talk so much at one time.

"Mr. Pickering?" I said softly. But his eyelids were getting lower and I could hear his breathing deepen. "Come on, Harvey," I whispered, and went to the door. Harvey got up reluctantly, like he was trying to choose between me and Mr. Pickering. "We'll come back," I promised.

Look at me, negotiating with a dog, I thought. But the deal must have sounded okay to Harvey, because he jumped down from the recliner as silent as a ninja. Mr. Pickering didn't even stir.

Chapter 17

Maggie

LOST DOG

Answers to Harvey
Male West Highland Terrier
Red harness, silver tag

If found, please call Maggie
555-621-1788

If you have ever lost a dog, you will understand how Maggie's body shakes when her mother tells her the truth about Harvey. For a moment, she is speechless with shock, and then a horrible sob erupts, the likes of which her mother has never heard come from her daughter.

"Oh, honey, I'm so sorry," she consoles her, but Maggie pushes her mother away.

"This is your fault!" Maggie shouts, racing to her room. "Harvey would never have been lost if we hadn't gone away!"

Slamming her door, Maggie throws herself onto her bed and lets loose gut-wrenching sobs that stain her pillow with tears. Losing Harvey is the worst thing that has ever happened to her.

An hour or so later, Maggie stomps downstairs and shoves a piece of paper into her mother's face. "We need to hang these up." It is a Lost Dog poster, and Harvey's sweet little face stares back at them. Below the photo is Maggie's mother's cell number.

Maggie's mother is in the middle of making lunch for the twins. The two little girls are already in their booster seats, eager for food.

"Where?" her mother asks.

"Everywhere. Anywhere. I don't care. I just want Harvey back!" Maggie's voice borders on hysteria. Her cheeks are flushed and her eyes sting from crying. Her mother's face softens.

"Okay," she agrees, ignoring the racket from the twins. "Here's what we'll do. We'll email the poster to your dad. He can print off a hundred copies at work. The twins can sleep in the car, and we'll put up the posters wherever you want. You'll need tape and a stapler."

Maggie exhales with relief. Maggie's mother rubs her daughter's shoulders and then pulls her in for a hug.

"Go send the poster to Dad and I'll get the twins ready," Maggie's mother says. With a plan in place, Maggie forces herself to think positively. If something bad had happened to Harvey, she would feel it in her bones—she's sure of it.

After sending a copy of the poster to her father, she makes a list of all the places she wants to hang them. She quickly realizes that a hundred posters is a lot. But she doesn't care. Even if it takes all day, she will paper the city with pictures of Harvey until he is found.

Chapter 18

Austin

As soon as I walked through the sliding doors at Brayside, Harvey bounded over. His tail was wagging so fast, all I could see was a blur.

Mary Rose was bustling around the counter. "Any word from his owner?"

"Not yet," I said, bending down to pat Harvey so I could avoid looking at her. I was sure Mary Rose would be able to tell if I was lying.

"Makes you wonder if something happened to his owner. Who wouldn't want him back? He's the sweetest thing." Then she added in a baby-talk voice, "Aren't you? Are you the sweetest?" Harvey moved toward her and sat, enjoying the attention while I stored my backpack and jacket in a locker.

"You're not going to believe this," Mary Rose said. "Mr. Pickering was asking when you were coming today." Mary Rose's voice was full of disbelief. "Said he had a story to tell you."

"Really?"

Mary Rose arched an eyebrow. "What's that all about?"

I shrugged my shoulders. "Not sure." But as soon as I turned away from Mary Rose, with Harvey at my heels, I smirked a little.

I wanted to get to Mr. Pickering's room before Grandpa could find me and give me a chore to do. I wasn't fast enough to escape Mr. Santos, though. He'd probably been waiting for me.

"Social media bird. Seven letters."

"Twitter." I answered so fast that even I was starting to think I was a crossword genius.

"Ha!" Mr. Santos said, and went back into his room to finish the puzzle.

As usual, it took Mr. Pickering a while to answer my knock. I pressed my ear to the door and listened. What if one day, he didn't come to the door? After all, he was ninety-six. I breathed a sigh of relief when the doorknob turned.

Harvey trotted in when the door opened and waited beside the recliner until Mr. Pickering settled himself down. Then he hopped up to join Mr. Pickering. Lots of residents at Brayside liked to ask me questions about my school or family, but Mr. Pickering didn't even say hello.

As soon as I was sitting on the couch, he turned to me. "Ever see a dust storm?" The way he said it made me wonder if he'd been thinking about it all day.

I shook my head. "Don't even know what one is."

"Like a blizzard, but instead of snow, it's sand and dirt stirred up from the ground. Summer of 1931 was the first year we had them. There's no way to describe what seeing that cloud on the horizon felt like. Stretching up from the ground to the sky like a mountain moving. There was nowhere to hide because the dust could get inside of anything—locked trunks, bags of flour, beds. It was like the land we'd lived off was attacking us. The storms would last for days. We'd be holed up in the house with wet rags over our mouths and noses to help us breathe.

"As soon as the field workers spotted the dust clouds, they would raise the alarm. We'd race to find safety in the house or the barn. Even the outhouse was better than being caught outside when a dust storm hit. Let me tell you, the sand and grit that got stuck up your nose and in your ears could suffocate a man.

"Everyone thought the dry summer of '33 would be the end of it, but '34 was even worse. I was eleven that year. The walk into town was like crossing a desert. On either side of the road, the fields were empty. The winds blew away the topsoil.

No one was getting a crop that year. Farmers lined up in town for relief. Bags of potatoes, carrots, turnips, fuel, and clothing were shipped in from all over the country. Even Mr. Hackett was feeling the pinch. His shelves lay empty. No point in buying goods no one could afford.

"Our farm was one of the luckier ones. My grandpa was smart to dig that pond. It provided us with enough water to keep Ma's garden and a few fields running. Along with the money Pa earned over the winter working in the bush, we never felt in danger like some of the families around us.

"Times were tough for Bertie, though. With no harvest, threshers weren't being hired. Her pa had moved to Weyburn to look for work, leaving Bertie on her own. I don't think she minded—she was part wild anyway. Maybe it was a relief to have him and his mean hands far away from her. But I saw worry wash over Ma's face when Bertie knocked on our door in the morning. Most times, she hadn't had anything to eat since Ma fed her the day before. She never asked for a handout. Bertie was too proud for that. Sometimes she'd come with a rabbit she'd snared or a fish she'd caught, and offer it to Ma, acting like she had a whole basketful at home. Truth was, there wasn't much left at her shack except for a tub to wash in and a bed. Whatever Bertie brought over was all that she had, but it was her way of repaying Ma.

"Ma wouldn't make a production of the offering. She'd fry it up or chop it into a stew and invite Bertie to join us.

Then Ma would send Bertie home with some extra biscuits and maybe a jar of jam or canned tomatoes if some were left in the pantry. It was like that back then—everyone helped each other. We might have been doing okay that summer, but who knew what the winter would bring, or next summer? It could be us out starving and our neighbors who were doing better.

"People made ends meet any way they could. Gophers had dug so many holes in the fields that now it wasn't just Pa who offered a bounty; the government did too. Rumor had it that the Minister of Agriculture paid out a thousand dollars in the first week. There were even recipes for gopher stew and gopher pie tacked up at Hackett's." Mr. Pickering laughed under his breath. "Didn't taste too bad, either. Or maybe we were hungry enough that we just didn't care.

"We'd all heard stories about hobos and tramps out looking for work and a place to sleep. Pa didn't want anyone stealing from us. He set me up in the barn with a shotgun and some water. It was my job to look after the animals and protect them every night. I'll admit it made me feel like a man knowing he trusted me like that. The twins begged to be allowed to stay with me, but Ma put her foot down and said I had enough to look after without the two of them as well. I think she knew I was getting to an age where I needed my space. Our two-bedroom house was cramped. Now that little Sylvia had moved out of Ma and Pa's room, three of us shared the big bed and the baby had her own cot. Amy was boarding at the convent school by then, so at least that was one less mouth to feed.

"This one day, I heard Bertie outside the cow barn. 'You awake?' she shouted. The rooster had only just crowed, so I didn't know what her rush was all about. I didn't have time to answer before she pulled open the barn door. Sunlight streamed in. I leaned over the edge of the loft, brushing hay off the side of my cheek. General stood up beside me and shook out his fur.

"'Am now.'

"'You gotta come see this,' she said.

"Bertie only had the one dress. Over the year, she'd grown, but the dress hadn't. It was so short, it hung a good two inches above her knobby knees. Bertie waited impatiently at the door while I climbed down the wooden ladder with General in my arms. We both stank of barn, but no one was wasting water on a bath that summer. We still went swimming in the creek, but now I had to be careful. I only went when the twins were busy with chores. You see, they'd taken up with Herbie Caldwell."

I raised my eyebrows in surprise. "The bully?"

"That's right. Davey had moved to the city with his folks, and that left an opening for Herbie's sidekick. Millard and Nigel were young, but their nasty side flourished under Herbie's care. I'd seen the mutilated carcasses of squirrels they'd killed and hanged from trees.

"I'd told Pa and he'd hollered at them good. Told them it was a waste of food, took away their slingshots for a week, and gave them extra chores. They'd both given me surly looks, but the twins had no proof it was me who'd ratted on them.

"I put General on the ground and he bounded outside to do his business. 'What's the big deal?' I asked. I could see the excitement on her face.

"'I gotta show you. Come on!' Bertie could run faster than most boys, including me. She took off across the yard with General racing behind. I wanted to yell at her to wait. I hadn't eaten breakfast yet or done my chores, but she was already halfway across our property.

"Bertie waited for me at the thicket by the stream. Nothing but a trickle of water sat in the bottom of the streambed. The bushes were coated with dust and looked half dead; dried-up leaves twirled on the branches, like they were begging to be dropped so the late August rains could come sooner. At least with the promise of winter, there'd be some relief from the dust storms. Maybe spring would bring a better crop—it was all anyone could talk about. The general consensus was that it couldn't get any worse.

"'You gonna tell me where we're going?' I asked. She'd stopped running, but now she walked quickly and didn't look back when she spoke. I had to run-walk to keep up with her.

"'It must have been buried till the dust storms dug it up.'

"'What was?'

"'Just follow me. You gotta see it.'

"So we went deeper into the bush, tramping over branches that snapped under our feet. I wished I'd stopped for a drink of water at the well before we left.

"The end of the bush marked the start of Richter's farm. They were in worse shape than we were. Shriveled crops lay in neat rows, the leaves crispy with lack of water. A breeze blew eddies of dust across the field. Bertie kept walking, carefully avoiding the plants, although at this point it wouldn't have mattered if she'd stepped on all of them. Mr. Richter wasn't getting anything out of his fields this year. All that seed and effort had gone to waste.

"'Where are we going?'

"'Not much farther.' Ma didn't let us go on other people's land, especially not sneaking around like this. I looked around in all directions, making sure we were alone. Ahead of me, Bertie stopped and pointed. 'I found it yesterday when I was setting snares for gophers.'

"Sticking out of the ground was something white. The dry soil blew up in a cloud around my shoes when I took a step closer. I still wasn't sure what she was so excited about. 'What is it?'"

As Mr. Pickering told the story, I leaned in, wondering the same thing.

"Bertie brushed some dirt away and I could see a smooth piece of bone. 'I think it's a skull.' I stepped closer, curious. Bertie dug deeper so more of the skull was exposed. We found animal bones all the time out in the field, but this wasn't from an animal. One look at the eye socket and I could tell it was human.

"'What d'ya say?' she asked, her face serious. 'Must have been here a long time.'

"Bertie and I set to scraping the soil away with our hands, like dogs. General watched us and started digging too, but we yelled at him to stop. The soil was so dry that as soon as it had been pushed away, it caved into the hole. Under the sandy layer, mud was packed hard like cement.

"'We need shovels.'

"'I don't have any,' she said.

"I sighed. Bertie's pa had been gone all summer. Looking for work on the trains, she said. But I'd heard Pa talking about it with the neighbors and calling men like Bertie's pa hobos. Whole gangs of men hopped trains and rode them up and down the tracks, stopping at towns and looking for work. They descended on towns like locusts, and it was only getting worse as more and more farmers left their dried-up land.

"'I'll go home,' I said and sighed again. I still hadn't had breakfast, and Ma would be livid if I didn't get my chores done. 'I wonder who it is.' Of course, my mind went to thinking we were solving a crime—an unsolved murder cracked by me and Bertie. I could almost see the reporter's camera flash popping in front of my eyes.

"Bertie shrugged. She peered into the hole and stuck her fingers in. 'Look at that.' At first, I thought it was a pebble.

But as she spat on it and rubbed the dirt away, I could see it was a bead. Small, round, with blue paint on it. 'There's more.' Bertie sifted her fingers through the loose soil and found another one. And then an arrowhead.

"I got chills, as if we were somewhere we weren't supposed to be. 'Maybe we should just leave it. Bury it back up.' I'd heard stories about curses following the dead. Bertie stared at the ground. As the wind blew across the field, a new torrent of dust was kicked up, and the tip of a different bone poked up through the earth.

Mr. Pickering looked at me. "You see, the prairie I'd known my whole life had changed over the last two summers. I didn't have blind trust anymore that it would provide for us. I was learning that the prairie wasn't the garden of Eden. It was harsh and unforgiving, maybe even vindictive. I shut my eyes against the stinging sand and shielded my mouth. I looked at the horizon. If a dust storm came now, we'd have nowhere to run. We'd be done for.

"I wanted to drag Bertie away. But I saw the look on her face. 'We need shovels.'

"'We could just leave it,' I suggested hopefully. Jamming a shovel into the hard-baked earth would be backbreaking. The sun was just cutting through the early morning haze on the horizon, but I could already tell it was gonna be a hot one. Just like every other day this summer.

"'No. That wouldn't be right. She's got to be reburied.'

"'How do you know it's a she?' I asked.

"Bertie held up the beads. 'Just a feeling I got.' I didn't point out there'd been an arrowhead too. 'We can't leave her like this. What if Herbie finds her? Or your brothers?'

"I didn't want to stay outside in the burning sun any longer than I had to. I knew from experience arguing with Bertie got me nowhere. 'All right, all right. I'll go back.' General sniffed the air and was about to follow me. 'Stay,' I told him, and he obeyed, going back to stand beside Bertie as if he knew his job was to guard her and the bones. I'd have to sneak back to the farm and get a shovel. If Ma caught me, she'd make sure I did my chores, and that would delay my return to Bertie by hours.

"The hens in the yard scattered as I walked toward the barn. Drops of sweat trickled down my back, and I thought how good it would feel to jump in the creek later. The drought had shrunk it to half its size, but it was wet and cool, so we didn't complain.

"I slid open the door of the barn and grabbed the shovel. The cows mooed at the interruption and I guiltily slunk away. Their udders would be swollen with milk. We were lucky that we still had the two cows. A lot of farmers around us had sold their livestock, happy to get the money now that the crops had been declared a disaster.

"Other farmers had lost their cattle to a growing pack of wild dogs. You see, the dogs were abandoned when their owners moved to the city, so the dogs turned feral, roaming across the farmland desert. I'd seen them once on the edges of our property. I'd called for Pa, and he'd shot off the gun to scare them away. Mangy-looking things. I almost felt sorry for them, at least from afar. Up close they were desperate and would tear a boy like me apart.

"I could hear Millard and Nigel shouting at each other from the other side of the house. The last thing I wanted was the two of them following me, so I ducked behind the well and waited until I heard them go inside. I raced across the yard and only slowed when I was hidden again in the thicket of bushes.

"Neither Bertie nor I were skilled trackers. But a mess of cracked branches and trampled grass made it easy for me to find my way back to her. General had lain down beside her, and she was patting his back. They both looked up when I walked across the field, the shovel swinging in my hands.

"'You should have brought water,' Bertie said. I felt a sinking in my gut. And food too. It would take a while to rebury the bones.

"'Didn't want Ma to see me.' Which was true. But if I'd been thinking clearly, I would have brought a bucket of water for us to share. Pa was always saying I didn't have any forward thinking; guess this was what he meant.

"'What if this whole field is a graveyard?' she said.

"The thought gave me a chill. We could be standing on someone's remains right now. 'Don't you think other bodies would have turned up?'

"'Maybe they did.'

"I imagined Mr. Richter plucking bones up out of the field like weeds and tossing them into a pile.

"'We need to dig a deeper hole and bury her properly,' Bertie said.

"I mopped my face with the tail of my shirt so she wouldn't see me grimace. Digging into the soil would leave me with blistered hands and an aching back. We should have been swimming right now, or at least doing chores so we could go swimming later. 'You sure?'

"Bertie nodded. 'This is her grave. We have to.'

"I took a deep breath and jammed the tip of the shovel into the ground. The impact jolted my arms and didn't give a bit. I dug the blade into a crack and loosened a piece. Bertie picked the chunk up with her hands and tossed it to the side. A wind blew up and we both pulled our collars up over our mouths and noses until it passed. I kept my eyes on the horizon, look-ing for an ominous black cloud. There wasn't one, but the distant ground was shimmering with heat already. I dug two more shovelfuls before Bertie pushed me aside. 'Go get water. I'll dig for a while.'

"I grabbed the shovel back and told her she should go get the water. 'If Ma catches me, I'll be stuck doing chores all morning.'

"Our argument went back and forth. By the time we saw Nigel, Millard, and Herbie approaching, it was too late to hide what we'd found.

"'What're you doing?' Nigel shouted. His words whipped at us in the hot, dry air.

"'Nothing. Just digging.' Which wasn't that unusual. When we'd been younger, we could entertain ourselves all day digging a hole deep enough to stand up in. They were like reverse tree houses. We'd use a rope to get in and out, or dig stairs into the side. Course, we always had to fill it up afterward too—that part wasn't as much fun.

"'In the middle of the field? This ain't your property.' Ever since Bertie had hit Herbie with that rock, he'd stayed clear of her. He got his digs in with me when he could, but I think he was afraid of her. Bertie wasn't like the other girls. Herbie didn't know what to make of her, or what to expect. He'd tried to insult her, but she just shrugged his comments off. The worst thing he could say to her was that she was poor and her pa was a hobo, which she knew was true. Watching her agree with his insults took all his power away, so eventually, he gave up.

"'We thought we might find a well.' My lie was weak. Everyone knew there wasn't water anywhere close to the surface. The water in our well had sunk so low we had to add more rope to the bucket to reach it. I wondered if there'd be a day when it was empty; as dried up as the land.

"The three boys laughed and came closer. General growled, sensing my discomfort. Behind me, Bertie kicked a chunk of dirt over the skull.

"'What'd you find?' Nigel asked, coming closer.

"'Nothing!' I shouted. The three of them surged forward and pushed me out of the way. Their eyes grew round as they spotted the skull.

"'Whoa! A body! You found a body!' They whooped and hollered, swarming around the bones like a murder of crows. Herbie grabbed the skull out of the ground and danced around with it, holding it above his head.

"'Put it back!' Bertie yelled.

"'Why? What do you care?'

"Nigel and Millard had started digging like gophers. The soil I had loosened gave way to what looked to be a leg bone. They held it up to show Herbie. 'There's arrow heads!' Nigel crowed, picking one up. 'This is a grave!' That started the three of them dancing and mimicking a war dance.

"Bertie's face went from shock to fury. Her lips curled and she glared at them. Then she looked at me. Her eyes darted to the shovel in my hand, a silent signal to use it.

"'Put it back,' I told them. 'We're going to bury it again.'

"'Why? It's no kin of ours.'

"'Doesn't matter.'

"The twins looked at each other and started laughing. Millard took the leg bone between his hands and posed like a baseball player. 'Batter up!'

"Herbie stood a few feet away with the skull in his hands, ready to pitch it to Millard. I watched them, feeling helpless and afraid to look at Bertie. A small part of me thought it was funny. If she hadn't been there, maybe I would have joined in. The bones had been in the ground for decades, maybe even centuries. There was no gravestone; no one was visiting or missing this person.

"I knew that it would be a waste of breath to tell them to put the bones back. Herbie wouldn't listen to me, and my brothers would follow his lead. Chances were good that he'd beat me up if I stood up to him. I didn't want my brothers to see Herbie whale on me. Or worse, watch as Bertie defended me.

"General barked a warning as Bertie ripped the shovel out of my hands. Her face was like a red-hot poker. I took a step away from her, and so did the twins. Herbie didn't have time to react. He probably didn't know what was coming.

"The shovel must have weighed almost the same as she did, but Bertie threw everything she had into it as she swung at Herbie. The back of it hit him across the ribs, and he went down like a hundred-pound sack of flour. Collapsed right in front of us. I thought we'd be digging another grave in that field.

"'Bertie!' I shouted. She dropped the shovel and looked at me, as shocked as I was. She bent down and scooped up the skull that had rolled out of Herbie's hand.

"'I told you to put it back.'

"I won't say I wasn't relieved to hear Herbie gasping for air, because I was. I thought she'd killed him.

"'Bertie!' I whispered.

"She shot me a murderous look. I worried that she'd pick up the shovel again. Millard held out the leg bone to her, his face a mix of awe and fear. He'd never seen anyone as fierce as Bertie. Even Ma in a lather couldn't hold a candle to Bertie Gamache.

"Herbie writhed in agony on the ground, gripping his ribs. I thought of all the times he'd cornered me on the playground and knew he deserved this agony. But still, to hear his whimpers pulled at me. Nigel and Millard stood gaping at Bertie.

"'Take him away, why don't you?' she said. 'He might have a broken rib or two.' The boys scurried to obey, a cloud of dust rising around them as they fell to the ground beside Herbie. Each of them grabbed an arm and tried to lift him, but that sent him screaming in more pain. Anyhow, his weight was no match for them. I wasn't sure who to go to—my brothers, who needed my help, or Bertie, who was unapologetically marching back to the grave.

"He's hurt real bad, Walter," Millard said. They'd pulled Herbie's shirt up. A bruise was already swelling around his middle. Bertie probably had broken a couple ribs and done who knew what else to him.

"Nigel piped up. 'He needs a doctor.'

"'He can't walk,' Millard added.

"I sighed. 'I'll go get the cart,' I said. Which meant explaining things to Ma and getting in all kinds of trouble. I cursed all four of them and shook my head.

"'Bertie,' I said, but she didn't look at me. She was kneeling over the bones, her head bowed.

"'Just go,' she said. 'I'll do this myself.'

"By the time I got home, confessed to Ma, tied the horse to the cart, and went back to Herbie, Bertie was no longer there. The skull was gone and so was our shovel. 'She's crazy as a loon,' Nigel whispered to me as we drove into town. Herbie was in the back, his head resting on Millard's lap.

"'No, she ain't,' I said with all the conviction I could muster.

"'All that for some stupid skull that's been lying in the dirt. What'd she care about it anyway?'

"'What if someone dug up the bones of our kin and started playing with them?' I said. 'How'd you feel about that?'

"Nigel pouted beside me. 'It wasn't our kin.'

"I didn't know why the bones had mattered so much to Bertie. I ran the events over in my head as we drove the miles to Herbie's home. I was sorry for Herbie, who kept moaning behind me in the cart. I thought Bertie was lucky she hadn't killed him.

"'You and Mill better stay away from Bertie for a while. She might still be sore about what happened. You understand?'

"Nigel nodded, and for the first time, I thought he might actually listen to me."

There was a long silence, and I could tell that Mr. Pickering was done.

"Wow," I breathed. I wasn't ready for the story to be over. I had questions about what happened next. Was Herbie hurt badly? Where did Bertie take the bones?

But I didn't speak up. One look at Mr. Pickering and I could tell that, just like last time, he was exhausted. At ninety-six, even telling a story could take it out of you.

"Come on, Harvey," I said, and headed to the door. Harvey stood, stretched, and jumped down to the floor.

Mr. Pickering's breath was deep and even. His mouth hung half-open. He was already asleep.

Chapter 19

Harvey

As Mr. Pickering shares his story with Austin, Harvey feels him tense. The subtle beat and throb of blood through his veins constricts, and Harvey senses the change. He's never been around someone as old as Mr. Pickering. The thick scent of him, heavy with life, lingers on Harvey's nose.

Harvey is content beside Mr. Pickering. He doesn't want to follow Austin when the boy signals it's time to leave, but he does. Cool air hits his belly when he rises.

He remembers the comfort of curling up on another bed, circling until he found the right spot. The sweet smell of her dreaming would fill his nose. Maggie. A memory of her dances just beyond him, and he feels a sudden pang as if he were very hungry. He remembers the way she would rub the scruff on his neck and tickle his ears. Her scent is gone now; he can't create it, but he could still identify it. As he trots behind Austin, the shadowy memory of his Maggie slips from him as quickly as it appeared—pushed aside by the smells littering the hallway carpet.

Chapter 20

Maggie

Across the city, Maggie and her mother have returned from the exhausting task of papering the neighborhood with posters. Eighty-six posters with a photo of Harvey and her mother's cell number have gone up in shopping centers, grocery stores, bus stops, schools, and community centers. Maggie brims with desperate hope that the phone will ring any minute.

"Can I take your phone with me?" she asks as she goes upstairs to brush her teeth and get ready for bed. "Someone might call in the night." Maggie's mother agrees. She is too tired to argue or explain that it is unlikely that anyone will phone so late.

Maggie brushes her teeth. The bathroom is directly over her father's office, and she can hear her parents talking through the air vent. Their voices are distant and echoing, but perfectly clear. "You shouldn't lead her on like this," her father says. "The dog's been gone for a week."

"You never know," her mother answers. Maggie can hear her sigh.

"It's a waste of time." Maggie feels her father's words like a punch to the gut. How can he just give up on Harvey?

Her mother's voice shakes. "If you'd seen her face when I told her—"

In the bathroom, Maggie gulps back tears. She has done a good job of keeping her fears at bay, but hearing her father's opinion sets her off. She thinks of little Harvey and how he used to curl up on her bed at night, fitting snugly in the crook of her knees. A wave of sorrow washes over her. She misses him utterly and completely. In all her twelve years, she has never felt such a loss.

What if one of the twins went missing? She knows her father wouldn't give up searching, no matter how hopeless it might seem. How can he think she'd give up on Harvey?

Maggie falls asleep with the phone on the pillow beside her, the ringer turned up to its highest volume.

There will be no messages when she wakes up on Tuesday morning, but she will have puffy eyes and a tear-stained face that she makes sure her father sees before he leaves for work.

Chapter 21

Austin

When Mr. Pickering opened the door the next afternoon, I wondered if he'd been sleeping all day. His white hair stuck up at the back and he was wearing pajamas and a robe. Harvey noticed the change too. Instead of trotting into Mr. Pickering's room like he lived there, he hung back, wary. Warning bells rang in my head, but I ignored them. Lots of people had lazy days.

"What's that dog doing here?" Mr. Pickering growled, eyeing Harvey.

I didn't answer right away, hoping his confusion would pass like last time. "This is Harvey. He loves to visit you." Harvey tilted his head when he heard his name.

Mr. Pickering harrumphed, took a few steps toward the recliner, and stared at Harvey as if trying to place him. Harvey took that as an invitation and trotted into the suite and up onto the recliner.

"General, get off the furniture," Mr. Pickering said.

"You mean Harvey," I corrected, and immediately wished I could bite my tongue. Grandpa told me it stresses old people out to be corrected. The last thing they want is to be reminded they're losing their memory.

A flash of recognition came over Mr. Pickering's face. "Yes. That's what I said." Then he looked at me suspiciously, and I knew he couldn't place me either.

"I'm Austin, Phillip's grandson," I said, and waited for him to answer. "I wanted to hear more about Bertie," I added, hoping to jog his memory.

"How do you know Bertie?"

The warning bells were getting louder—more like sirens, actually. "I don't. You've just told me some stories. I'm curious to know what happened after you found the grave and she hurt Herbie."

The confusion on Mr. Pickering's face cleared. His shoulders fell down from around his ears and he made it the rest of the way to the recliner. Harvey jumped down to make room for him and then leaped back up when the old man was settled. It was like the two of them had been friends forever.

"Was Herbie okay in the end?"

Mr. Pickering frowned. "He was laid up for weeks after Bertie swung at him. I told you we'd found the skeleton?" he asked. I nodded. "Well, Ma was fit to be tied when she found out that we'd been digging in another man's field. Ma put us to work hauling water to what was left of her garden. Guess she thought giving us chores from dawn to dusk would keep us out of trouble."

"What about Bertie?"

"Didn't see her much for the rest of the summer. Figured she'd moved the skeleton though, because I found the shovel leaning against the cow barn a few days later." Mr. Pickering shook his head. "Must have taken her days to dig through that soil.

"The twins tattled on Bertie, telling Ma the whole story about how she'd swung at Herbie. Guess they enjoyed that they were blameless for once. Ma wouldn't let me see Bertie after that. Called her a loose cannon and said she had poor breeding. Truth be told, I was relieved. What I'd seen in Bertie that day had scared me too. I suppose Bertie figured she was in a mess of trouble, because she didn't come around after that. She was probably still mad at me for taking Herbie back home.

"I figured I'd see her when school started. The class had shrunk to only a handful. So many families had moved away because of the drought." He paused. "I told you about the drought?"

I nodded. "In '33 and '34, right?"

"Grain prices had gone down to nothing. Even if the crops had been good, it wouldn't have made much of a difference. Pretty much everyone in Wilcox was on relief. As soon as he could, Pa went off to the bush to work for the lumber company. To be honest, we were relieved to see him go. The summer had been hard on him and he was a bear most nights, yelling at one of us boys for the smallest thing." Mr. Pickering broke off. When he started up again, his voice was different, quieter.

"One night I caught him sobbing at the kitchen table. Ma stood over him, rubbing his back as his shoulders quaked. I'd never seen my pa cry. Ma glanced up in time to see me disappear behind the door. She didn't speak of it the next morning, but the air in the house had shifted. Ma was holding all of us together. The weight of the family rested on her shoulders; I wondered how she didn't crack under the pressure."

Mr. Pickering took a deep breath. His eyelids were heavy. "Mr. Pickering?" I said quietly, ready to take Harvey and leave.

But then his eyes snapped open. "We survived '34 and everyone was relieved when fall arrived. There was talk that we'd have an easy winter, that Mother Nature would take pity on us after the drought." He laughed ruefully, which made me think that wasn't what happened.

"Our teacher that year was… Miss Hayward, I think. She was young and pretty, and I didn't think she'd last long. Someone would ask her to get married, and then we'd start all over with a new one. It had happened plenty. During my schooling, I had at least eight teachers.

"We'd been in school for about a month when Bertie showed up. I hadn't seen her since the day Herbie got hurt. Herbie's jaw dropped when she walked in.

"My stomach flipped when I saw Bertie. A whole lot of things ran through my head. 'Hey there, Bertie,' I said, twisting around in my desk to talk to her. 'How've you been?' I pretended like things between us were normal, even though I knew they weren't.

"She was even skinnier than before. I wanted to think her pa had come back for her and got her fed and set up right with help from relief. But seeing the way her cheekbones stuck out, I knew that wasn't what had happened.

"'Getting by' was all she said, which was no answer at all. There was a haunted look to her that left me cold. I wanted to blame her pa or even Herbie and the twins, but I knew that'd be a lie. I was the one who abandoned her in the field that day. She hadn't been around because of me.

"I sat there the whole morning, working up the courage to try to win her over at lunch. But then a baseball game got started and I was asked to pitch. I'd been planning to offer her a ride back with us, as a way to make peace. Ma had let me take Victor and the cart to school. But as I led the horse out of the school barn, Bertie left the yard without so much as a backward glance in my direction.

"The whole day, Nigel and Millard had given Bertie a wide berth, watching her movements like a couple of scared mice. It was a nice change, to be honest. The twins and I were at each other's throats constantly—at school and at home. Anything was an excuse to battle. Our scraps were usually harmless, but Nigel and I got into it most often. I tell you what—he was a sneaky one. I caught him raiding the cellar or sloughing off his chores more than once. With Pa gone, it fell on me to discipline Nigel. Ma was busy with Sylvia, looking after the three of us, and running the farm. Half the time, she turned a blind eye to his antics. But I couldn't.

"'Bertie!' I hollered, once I'd hitched Victor to the wagon.

"'What're you thinking, offering her a ride?' Nigel growled at me. 'Ma doesn't want us near her, not after what she did to Herbie.'

"I wasn't sure Ma still felt that way, but I knew Nigel would be certain to tell her I'd given Bertie a ride home if it meant getting me in trouble. Bertie never turned around anyway, so I snapped the reins and off we clambered down the dry dirt road. But the whole way, I was thinking that I should've gone after her, tried harder to give her a ride.

"When we got home, the twins dropped their lunch pails and ran off with their slingshots. They were hoping to hit some squirrels. Mr. Friedman, who was a furrier, had started coming to Wilcox once a month. Mr. Hackett would sell pelts to him for three cents a piece and give us two—a small fortune to us boys.

I put Victor out in the paddock and went to find Ma. She was busy in the kitchen, with Baby Sylvia underfoot, as usual.

"'Ma?' I said.

"She turned to me, a lump of dough in her hands. Her long brown hair was always tucked up with pins at the base of her neck. A few strands had escaped, and she wiped them away with the back of her hand. 'What is it, Walt?' She began rolling out the dough on the kitchen table.

"I tell you, I didn't know where to begin, but my window of opportunity was closing. Sylvia or the boys would demand attention in a minute and I'd be left with the question hanging off my tongue. 'It's Bertie.'

"Her eyes flickered to my face and back to the dough.

"'She came to school today. She—' I broke off. By now, we all knew what hunger felt like. But now I knew what it looked like too. 'Could I take her some food? I don't think she has much.'

"Even as I said the words, I knew we didn't have much either. And what we did have had to get all five of us through a winter. But Ma paused in her rolling and looked at me. 'Is her pa back yet?'

"I shrugged.

"'You think she's all alone out there?'

"I shrugged again.

"Ma lost her patience. 'Well, find out, for heaven's sake! We can't afford to feed another mouth, but I'm not about to let the poor girl starve. Yes, take her something from the cellar, but be mindful.' Ma set her mouth and went back to rolling the dough.

"The cellar door was to the left of the stove. I opened it and climbed down the ladder to the dirt floor. Pa had built rows of shelves all along the walls, and Ma had been busy canning and preserving what she could. It looked like a lot now, but as the winter wore on, the shelves would empty and we'd be eating canned turnips and bread for dinner again. Or not. Pa had given me free rein with the shotgun and told me it was time I got hunting. He'd taken me over to a neighbor's and I'd tried my hand at skinning and carving a deer. Let me tell you, there was no better smell than a venison steak frying on the stove.

"Against the wall sat an empty burlap sack. I grabbed it and put in some potatoes and onions and a jar of pickles. Most of the blueberries I'd picked that summer had been made into pies, but there were a few jars of pie filling Ma planned to use later. I put one of those in too.

"As I slung the sack over my shoulder and climbed out of the cellar, Ma nodded to a fresh-baked loaf of bread on the counter. 'Bring her half of that. We need the rest for breakfast.' I did as I was told and set off across the yard with the bag of food and General bounding along beside me.

"'Where're you going?' Millard called.

"'To Father Perrin's,' I lied. 'Ma wants him to have this.' Hearing the priest's name stopped the two of them dead in their tracks, and they went back to squirrel hunting.

"I'd seen Bertie's house from afar, but I hadn't had a reason to get up close to it in all the time we'd been friends. The shack was tucked into a small clearing, with the creek—if you could call it that—running beside it. A mishmash of wood and tin siding had been used for the walls, and the roof looked ready to cave in.

"'Bertie?' I called as I entered the yard. It was quiet. A clothesline was strung up, but there was nothing on it. A chair with a busted leg rested against the side of the house. I walked up to the window and peeked inside. One pane of glass was broken and I heard her voice before I saw her.

"She was chatting away. I thought maybe she had a visitor and that was why she hadn't heard me coming. I scanned the room to see who else was there. It was empty. Bertie sat on the floor, pretending to sew. She pinched her fingers together and pulled an imaginary needle through invisible fabric. 'There now! Isn't that better! You'll be so much warmer this winter,' she said, and held up the imagined shirt. 'Let me put it on you.' She went through the motions of dressing a person who wasn't there and stood back to admire her handiwork.

"I watched in shock as the one-sided conversation continued. She'd been alone in the woods all summer, and there had been nothing standing between her and madness. I'd abandoned her. Her pa was gone. She'd probably had nothing to eat but what she could forage on her own. General looked up at me, wondering why we weren't moving. I set the sack down on the doorstep.

"You know, I didn't call out to her. Guess I was afraid of being so close to someone no longer in her right mind. I tore out of her yard, with General hot on my heels. I never told anyone about that day. Ma asked later about Bertie, but I lied and said she wasn't home."

When Mr. Pickering finished, I couldn't think of anything to say. He'd been carrying that story around his whole life. All of a sudden, a whole bunch of things about getting old made sense to me, like a picture coming into focus. At ninety-six, he had a chance to unload some of his memories. Maybe that's why he was telling them to me.

Harvey sat quietly beside Mr. Pickering through the whole story, but now he got up and stretched, his long, pink tongue curling as he yawned. I thought I should say something, but I didn't know what.

"Turn on the weather channel, will you? And ask Mary Rose to bring me some dinner. I'm too tired to go to the dining room."

"Okay," I said, and called Harvey, who jumped to the floor.

"Let General out, will you?" he murmured.

This time, I didn't bother to correct him.

Chapter 22

Maggie

There were no calls about Harvey on Tuesday. Maggie was allowed to stay home to wait by the phone, but now it is Wednesday, and Maggie's mother has told her she has to go to school.

"You've already missed a week," Maggie's mother says. "I'll call the school if I hear anything, I promise."

Maggie sits glumly at the breakfast table. She feels like the life has been sucked out of her. How will she ever have fun again? Laughing feels like a betrayal to Harvey. School, where her friends will want to hear all about her trip, will be painful. She doesn't think she can put on a brave face.

When they pull up to school, Maggie reluctantly passes the phone back to her mother. "You'll call the school if someone calls?"

"Yes, I promise."

Maggie hesitates before getting out of the car. She can see her friends standing on the front steps waiting for her. She notices that Lexi got a new haircut while she was gone. Normally, she'd rush to be with them, eager to talk about her trip and gush about Lexi's hair. But how can she pretend to be excited when Harvey is missing? She'll have to tell them, she realizes. All of a sudden, she doesn't think she can leave the car.

"Mom?" She turns away from the window. She can feel a lump in her throat and isn't sure how to get rid of it. Her chin trembles.

Maggie's mother puts her hand on her daughter's arm. "It'll be okay. We'll find him."

Maggie doesn't tell her mother about overhearing her parents' talk the other night, or the doubts that have started to creep in. Harvey might be lost for good. And worse, they might never know what happened to him.

"I'm not sure I can go up there." She wants to go home and curl up on her bed.

Maggie's mother gives her hand a squeeze. "Yes, you can. There's no point sitting around at home waiting for a call. Being at school will take your mind off things."

Her friends are talking together, probably wondering why she isn't getting out of the car. It all feels too overwhelming. Maggie knows that she can't think about it; she has to just go—like ripping off a Band-Aid.

"You'll feel better once you're there. It's the thinking about it that's so hard."

Maggie blinks away the tears and takes a deep breath. Gripping her backpack straps in one hand, she opens the car door and is hit with a gust of wintry air. "Bye, honey!" her mother calls. "I love you." Maggie shuts the door without turning around.

"When did you get back?" Brianne asks.

"Two days ago," she admits. "But late at night. We needed to sleep in yesterday. And then—" She breaks off, not sure how to continue. "Something horrible happened." She doesn't mean to make a dramatic pause; she's trying to keep her voice even. "Harvey's lost."

The girls howl in protest.

"When?" Lexi asks.

"H-how?" Brianne stammers.

"The day after we left!" A surge of anger hits Maggie. She's kept it at bay, but now it comes at her full force. "The stupid dog sitter didn't know the gate was open."

There is a chorus of "That's terrible!" and "No!"

"We can help you look for him after school," Brianne offers.

Maggie shakes her head. If only it were that simple. "We

looked all day yesterday and put up posters. But it's been so long. He could be anywhere." She blinks back the tears that prickle behind her eyes.

"I'll bet someone took him. A dog thief or someone. You should tell the police." Lexi loves conspiracy theories, so Maggie is not surprised by this suggestion.

"I just want to know he's okay," Maggie says tearfully. Her friends wrap their arms around her, commiserating.

Maggie stumbles through her day, doing her best to concentrate during class. She visits the office three times to check for a message from her mother, but each time, the secretary shakes her head. After school, Maggie does her homework and eats dinner with her mother's cell phone by her side. But it never rings. When Maggie goes to sleep, she does so with a heavy heart.

Harvey is still lost.

Chapter 23

Austin

"Still haven't heard from Harvey's owners?" Grandpa said when the two of us were walking home from Brayside on Wednesday.

"Nope. Nothing." Which was true. I hadn't heard anything.

Grandpa made a noise in his throat that meant he had more to say on the topic. "He belongs to someone. Don't you get too attached to him; it'll just make it harder to give him up."

Too late, I thought. Mom felt the same as me, even though she tried to act like she didn't. Every day when I walked into the apartment with Harvey, she said hello to me and gave Harvey a belly rub. I checked online at school to see how much

Westie dogs cost. A lot. More than Mom and I would ever be able to afford. The only way we'd get a dog like Harvey was by me finding one.

Harvey strained on his leash, pulling me toward a fire hydrant. You'd think he had to put out a fire the way he yanked to get there. I let him sniff around for the right spot to pee. It was getting dark out earlier and earlier now. His white coat was bright against the gray sidewalk and buildings.

"He's good for the old people," I said. "Like Mr. Pickering. He talks to me now."

Even under the streetlights, I could see the *I-told-you-so* in Grandpa's expression. "I thought Walt scared you." Grandpa called everyone by their last name when he was at work, but as soon as we left for the day, he talked about them as if they were all on a first-name basis.

"He does scare me a little. Well, he did." I thought about the farm and Bertie and General. When he was talking about them, I forgot he was old Mr. Pickering. I started seeing him as the boy in the pictures in his photo collage. "He's not so bad."

Grandpa nodded and ruffled my hair. Harvey pulled and dragged me over to a tree, sniffing like his life depended on it. *Do dogs ever run out of pee?* I wondered.

"Not sure how much longer Mr. Pickering will be on his own," Grandpa said. "I think he'll get moved up to the second floor pretty soon."

This news gave me a jolt. "Why?"

"Guess his heart is giving him some trouble, and he's getting confused. He's ninety-six, after all. He's not going to live forever."

"He looks fine," I said. But the truth was, there had been times when he put a hand on his chest and winced. I'd seen all the pills that he had to take. And sometimes he forgot to go to the dining room for meals and Mary Rose had to remind him. Grandpa's warning left a bad taste in my mouth.

"He'd hate it on the second floor," I blurted.

"It's for his own good."

I scowled at Grandpa. He didn't know Mr. Pickering like I did. Up on the second floor, he wouldn't be allowed to come and go as he pleased, because there's a secret code to the elevator. Nurses come around to give out medication and the old people have to be supervised when they shower. None of the rooms have kitchens—just a bed and a little sitting area with a TV. Mr. Pickering wouldn't be able to make his toast and tea. And what about Harvey? Were dogs even allowed up there?

"I still don't know how General lost his leg," I mumbled to Grandpa. Grandpa's arm went around my shoulder. Instead of it making me feel better, it made me sad, because all of a sudden I realized that Grandpa won't be around forever either.

Chapter 24

Harvey

Harvey bounds in from the outdoors and Austin bends down to remove some dried-up leaves tangled in his fur. The air has turned chilly. A change is coming—Harvey can sense it.

Austin holds Harvey's chin in his hands. Their eyes meet. "You're happy here, aren't you?" he whispers. Harvey tilts his head at the boy, curious about the shift in his voice. Harvey licks Austin's hand and gives it a sniff, but detects nothing out of the ordinary. When the boy stands up, his footsteps are slow and tentative, so Harvey follows suit, subduing himself. He has learned to read his people and follow their behavior.

Harvey can read signs the same way a good ratter tracks his prey. Something tells him that he needs to be alert, and he pricks his ears as he follows the boy down the hallway.

Harvey assumes he is going to his favorite room, and sure enough, Austin stops in front of it and raps on the door. He can already smell the muskiness, the lived-in quality of the room that makes him want to burrow in deep, from under the door.

Harvey raises a paw and scratches the door, but Austin quickly says, "No." A *yip* then, to let Mr. Pickering know they are waiting. That is also met with a "Shush" from Austin. Harvey hears the familiar sounds of Mr. Pickering making his way to the door. It clicks and Harvey gets a whiff of the delicious slippers that he'd love to sink his teeth into. Mr. Pickering can't quite bend all the way down to pat Harvey on the head; but he tries, his fingers dangling in Harvey's direction. Harvey ignores the fingers and trots inside—underskirt swaying thanks to a satisfactory grooming by Artie—to find his spot on the recliner.

"Harvey wanted to say hello," Austin says. That much is obvious since Harvey is already seated on the recliner, patiently waiting for Mr. Pickering to join him.

Harvey can tell that the old man is rested. He moves without hesitation and his voice is more robust. Harvey nestles into the slot between the man's arm and the chair's armrest. He is content. He rests his chin on his front paws and looks around the room. Harvey sighs. He feels the man pat his head, stroking the space between his ears. His hands fall heavily and lack the vigor of a younger person's, but the knobby fingers know how to get in the space just under his ear and on the side of his neck, just the way someone else used to. The memory bursts into his head for only a second and then disappears. Without smells to connect his past and his present, the someone flutters away.

Harvey smells the sour saltiness of Austin, who sits across from him. There are a hundred other scents that linger on Austin's clothes and shoes; he is coated with other people and places.

The old man's voice fills his ears.

"The rest of that winter was rough. Maybe it was because Pa was gone and I was old enough to know about the hardship we were enduring. Or maybe that winter really was a worse winter than the others.

"I didn't go to school much because there was too much work to do around the farm. I took to sleeping in the cow barn again. And I'd go out almost daily to leave something on Bertie's doorstep. Don't know if she figured out that it was me who was leaving it, but she never said anything the few times I showed up at school.

"I took Pa's shotgun with me whenever I left the farm. One of our neighbors killed a deer, so Ma sent me to trade some of her chickens for the meat. Her cellar was no match for the three of us growing boys. We went to bed hungry a lot of nights, but I got used to it. Everyone was in the same predicament.

"Although Bertie had it the worst.

"Usually, when I left something for her on the steps, I'd do it quick and hope she didn't see me.

"She hadn't been to school for a while when I went to her shack to check in on her one afternoon. The snow had fallen and a thin blanket covered the ground. There was no smoke rising from her chimney and I wondered if she'd left the shack altogether. Maybe her pa had finally come back for her and they'd moved to another place. But footprints near the door told me she was still living there after all.

"'Bertie?' I called out. I peeked into her window, scraping the frost off with a fingernail. 'Bertie?' I called again. I didn't see anything at first, but then a shape moving in the corner caught my eye. A dark lump was rocking back and forth, tucked in the corner.

"I burst through the door. The cabin was as cold as the outside, and I could see my breath come out in puffs as I bent down to check on her. She had a thin quilt wrapped around her shoulders. I crouched down to look into her eyes. She stared through me, limp hair falling over her face.

"'Bertie!' I gasped. I grabbed her shoulders, shocked to feel nothing but bones. A shiver ran through her like a convulsion. Panic filled me and all at once I knew she was going to die here. She was too weak to leave. I scooped her up like a child—she probably weighed the same as little Sylvia. I carried her out into the snow-covered yard. General sniffed her feet, barely covered in the same leather shoes she'd always worn, and raised sorrow-filled eyes to me. Maybe he could smell her frailness. The fiery wild thing that she had been was no more.

"I shouldered my way through the brush. Branches ripped at my face and clothes, snapping off and falling underfoot. I held Bertie's face against my chest. I could feel her breath rattling through her ribs. All I knew was that I had to get her home. Ma would know what to do. She'd lay her down in the bed and cover her with a quilt and spoon hot broth into her mouth.

"Darkness had started to fall as I made my way across our yard. Home was close. Let me tell you, my heart was pounding with the effort—and with fear. In the distance, I heard howls. General stopped, hackles raised. He barked back in a ferocious answer to the call, and started to move away from me. I'd seen the dog pack a few times that winter, always in the distance. Once, I found what was left of a kill and stared at the head of a young doe jealously. The pack was growing. They would be after the same game that I was.

"'General, come!' I bellowed. The gun was slung over my back, and I couldn't reach for it with Bertie in my arms if trouble came.

"At the sound of my voice, Bertie began to murmur nonsense. 'It'll be okay,' I huffed as we passed the well and one of Ma's gardens. A few sticks poked up through the snow. 'We're almost there,' I said, more for me than for Bertie.

"'Ma!' I shouted on the doorstep. General barked and pawed at the door. 'Ma!' Honestly, I wanted to cry with relief that we'd made it. I knew Bertie wasn't out of the woods yet, but at least she'd be safe and warm.

"Ma opened the door and a blast of heat hit me. The wood stove was on and I'd never been so relieved to step inside my home. 'I found her like this,' I panted.

"Ma's eyes widened when she took a look at the limp pile in my arms. Bertie's skin was so pale, it was almost gray. The space under her eyes was puffed up and purple. Ma pulled me inside and shut the door after me. She directed me to her bed and set to work. I stood by helplessly, watching as she layered quilts over Bertie and heated hot-water bottles.

"Seeing me doing nothing, Ma said, 'Go to the well.' It was a relief to have a job. I grabbed the bucket and went back outside. General was waiting for me and stayed close beside me as I walked across the yard. Already my tracks had almost been covered by the snow. One dog howled again. Then another.

A chill ran through me. They were getting closer. I put a hand down on General, a silent order to stay close."

The old man stops. Harvey lifts his chin, aware of the change. Across from him, Austin sits on the edge of couch, his whole body tense as he leans forward.

"All these years later, I still wonder how much of it had been my fault. Bertie could have died in that shack. I'd abandoned her when she needed me most. As I trudged toward the well, guilt formed a lump in my throat and I fought back tears. Bertie was sleeping when I got back to the house. Ma had started a kettle, and it whistled on the stove. She came out of her room and shut the door gently behind her.

"'Is she going to be okay?' I asked.

"'She's starved half to death,' Ma said, shaking her head. She looked at me as if she had more questions, but she didn't ask them. I grabbed my woolen hat and a warmer coat, and went back outside. General trotted over and followed me toward the barn. Ma would sleep with the twins tonight and let Bertie have her bed. The best thing I could do was stay out of the way.

"I waited till I was up in the loft to let my tears fall. They came all of a sudden in a flood, and I didn't try to stop them. I kept thinking about that day we walked back from town, when Bertie had told me I was the best friend she'd ever had.

"I'd let her down, leaving her alone in the shack. My selfishness, or my stupidity, turned me blind to how much she needed me. She could have died. I burrowed my face into General's fur. He lay beside me as all the shame and regret spilled out of me."

Chapter 25

W hen Mr. Pickering was done, I cleared my throat, but my words still came out thick. "That's so sad." The old man moved a hand to his chest and winced. Harvey hadn't moved from his spot, but he raised his head and looked at Mr. Pickering.

"Could you get me a glass of water?" Mr. Pickering asked, his voice hoarse.

"Sure," I said, but by the time I came back with a glass, Mr. Pickering was snoring lightly, his mouth hanging open.

I wished he hadn't fallen asleep. I wanted to know what happened next. Was Bertie okay? Did she stay with them? I put the glass on the table in case he wanted it when he woke up. I patted my thigh, a signal to Harvey that we should leave.

As soon as Harvey stood up, Mr. Pickering was startled awake. "General!" he gasped.

"No, Mr. Pickering. It's me and Harvey." I put my hand on his shoulder to settle him.

He looked at me, confused. "Where's Bertie?"

"She's at the farm," I said gently. "Remember? You rescued her." It seemed like the kindest thing to say.

He rubbed his forehead. "Oh yes. And then she moved in with us."

"You looked after her."

"I would have done anything for her," he said.

I passed him the water. He took a few sips and then passed it back to me, so I could put it on the table. "Thank you," he mumbled.

"I'll let you rest." I turned to the door.

"No," he said. "Stay. I like the company."

Maybe I should have gone; he was old and looked worn out from all the talking. But I still hadn't found out how General lost his leg. "You sure you're not too tired?"

"Sit," he said, and waved at the couch. So I did, and Harvey joined me for a change.

"Bertie got her strength back slowly. She stayed with us through the winter. Ma couldn't let her go back to the shack on her own. Bertie was in no condition to go anyway. She wore what clothes we had left of Amy's.

"While Bertie got stronger eating Ma's food, she helped look after Sylvia. I think Bertie would have rather gone hunting in the bush or ice fishing with me and the twins. But she was indebted to Ma and knew she was needed in the house. The role didn't fit her well. I heard her tell Sylvia about outrunning wild dogs and battling black bears—stories that would have made Ma's jaw drop.

"It was late February, and bit by bit the days were getting longer. The spring thaw was just around the corner and the mood on the farm was relaxing. We'd almost made it through another winter.

"'Where're you off to?' Bertie asked me as I dumped my plate in the washtub after our midday dinner. I saw the wistful look on her face and knew that she'd rather be tramping around in the forest than stuck in the house with Ma and Sylvia.

"The shotgun hung on its hook by the door, and I nodded in its direction. 'Going to see if I can catch that fox that's been poking around.' The last thing we needed was a fox stealing Ma's baby chicks when they were born in the spring. Besides, a fox sniffing around made the cows nervous. Keeping both cows happy was our prime goal. We'd had milk all winter and Ma had made a deal with a neighbor to breed one of them in the spring.

"I was old enough now to realize how much work Ma had to do with Pa gone so much. I wondered if she didn't ever get mad at him for saddling her with the farm while he went into the bush. It was probably hard work keeping the books for the lumber company—and keeping the rough men who worked there happy—but it meant an escape from the chores and drudgery of feeding and caring for all of us.

"'You want to come?' I asked Bertie. Her face lit up. The sun was high and sharp in the blue sky. I'd gotten used to being on my own and, truth be told, kind of liked it.

"You know," Mr. Pickering paused, considering something, "I probably took after Pa that way. I could see how being in the bush all winter appealed to him. Being left alone with my thoughts was a luxury.

"Well, I guess Ma saw the look on Bertie's face. 'Just go,' she muttered from the stove where she was cooking stew from the rabbits I'd snared a couple of days before. Bertie had skinned the rabbits and we left the meat to hang in the barn, where it froze solid. There were still onions and carrots stored in the cellar, and Ma added those too, along with some chicken broth and salt and canned tomatoes.

"Bertie didn't wait to be told twice. We put on a couple layers of woolen long underwear and then our leather boots—mine were hand-me-downs from Pa, and Bertie shared hers with Ma. We pulled on hand-knit hats and mitts, and tied scarves tight around our faces. By the time we were done getting ready, only a sliver of space for our eyes was left. I grabbed the gun and slung it over my shoulder. I liked how it felt smacking against my legs as I walked into the cold.

"General came bounding after us, and I tossed him half a biscuit I'd saved from dinner. He ran after it, snuffling in the snow crystals to dig it up.

"'Should be starting to melt soon,' Bertie said. The sun was warm and I pulled the scarf down to my chin. Each step we took cracked through the icy top layer of snow. "You mind if we head over that way?" Bertie pointed toward where her shack was.

"I didn't say anything, but I was surprised. I thought she'd want to avoid that place. There was nothing there but bad memories.

"'I should check on it. Make sure it's still standing. Empty.'

"It was her last word that made me pause. 'If he'd come back, he would've been by looking for you.'

"Her eyes went cold. I knew as well as she did that most farm dogs were treated with more care than she got from her pa.

"'If you're wondering where he is,' I continued, 'we could ask Officer Reginald to find out. He could send word to another detachment." Officer Reginald, or Reggie, as we called him, was the officer stationed in Weyburn. He came out to check on us, especially Ma, during the winter. He was from down East and was continually surprised by the bitter cold and how Ma was able to run the farm while Pa was in the bush.

"'I did ask him.'

"Her news caught me off guard. 'You never said.What'd you find out?'

"She hesitated so long, I thought maybe she wasn't going to tell me. Her face had that haunted look I saw so often. 'He spent last winter on the trap lines, then he went down to Prince Albert. Spent a bit of time in jail during the summer and couldn't find anything else after that.'

"'Maybe he got a job.'

"Bertie snorted. 'What kind of a job? Everyone's looking for work. I don't think they'd pick a drunk like him over a man with a family, do you?'

"'S'pose not,' I muttered.

"'I don't know what's worse. That he *is* dead, or that he isn't and just doesn't care a lick about me.'

"I couldn't stand to let Bertie think that way, so I lied. 'You know how times are, Bert. He might be trying to get back to you, but with no money and the winter…' I let my voice drift off. 'Anyhow, you're safe with us. Ma likes having you around.'

"'What about when your pa comes back? He won't want another mouth to feed, 'specially if this summer is anything like the last one.'

"I didn't want to admit it, but she was right. 'Don't worry about that stuff right now,' I told her, and started moving ahead through the snow. It was a chicken's way to answer, brushing the problem aside like it didn't matter. The thing was, our lives were in a constant state of wondering about the future; trying to predict what was coming had become a full-time hobby for all of us.

"As we moved through the bush, I kept an eye out for tracks and movement in the bushes. In my mind, I'd already made a hat out of the fox pelt. I wanted Herbie Caldwell to drool over the bushy tail hanging down my back when I showed up to school with it. Or better yet, I could sell it to Mr. Friedman and buy us a new radio. The one we had was always cutting out with static in the evening.

"The dog raced ahead of us. He needed to stay by my side or I'd have no luck catching anything. 'General!' I called. Instead of seeing him come bounding back, we heard a high-pitched yelp and a howl of pain.

"'General?' I shouted again. Bertie was already running toward the sound, her too-large boots clomping through the icy snow. I caught up to her quickly and forged ahead.

"General was lying on the ground, his legs twisted behind him. He was licking his front paw. Before I got any closer, I could see what had happened. The jaw of a leg-hold trap was clamped around his right front leg."

"Bertie stopped beside me. 'What do we do?' she cried.

"'Hey, General,' I said softly. I didn't want him to move and make the trap spring tighter on his leg. 'Hey, there, boy. We're here.' General lifted his head and whined. I passed the shotgun to Bertie and walked in a wide circle so he'd be able to see me approach. General went back to licking his leg, but I could see blood seeping into the snow around him. The trap's teeth had sunk deep into his flesh, probably all the way to the bone.

"Bertie hung the gun up on a tree branch and followed in my tracks. 'What do we do?' she asked again.

"I moved closer to General and lifted his head away from his leg. I needed to see how bad the damage was. If we got the trap off, would he be able to walk? General looked at me with sorrowful eyes. His whine had changed to a whimper of pain. His fur was matted with blood. Sure enough, the teeth of the trap had pierced through to the bone—I could see the white of it exposed and sticking out at an odd angle.

"'Leg's broken.' I couldn't look at General, knowing how bad it must be hurting. For his sake, I hoped the shock would set in quick.

"Bertie tore off her hat and crouched beside me. 'We have to get him free.'

"'Bertie,' I started. She knew as well as I did that on a farm, a dog with a broken leg was usually put down. It was easier to get another one than to heal an injured animal. Plus, the trap was an old one, covered in rust.

"I stood staring at General's leg and the way the trap's serrated teeth had bit clear to the bone. I knew I couldn't leave him there. It was up to me to help him, but I didn't know what to do. I wished my pa were here.

"'Walt!' Bertie slapped my arm. Her eyes were blazing. 'Do something!'

"'Hold his head,' I said to Bertie. She moved closer to him and put a hand on his head. She stroked him behind the ears, the way he liked. He whimpered, as if pleading with us to help him. Bertie wrapped both arms around his neck and held him tight. I stood up and put my feet on the release mechanism on either side of the clamp. But my weight wasn't enough. The rusty metal levers wouldn't budge. I wrestled with them until my fingers were numb and bleeding, coated with rust.

"I stood up and weighed our options. The trap was chained to a tree, so we weren't going to be able to carry him home with the trap still on his leg. Our only choice made my stomach turn. Bertie held on to General, her hand buried in his thick winter coat.

"'I'm gonna have to go home and get an ax,' I said.

She looked at me and shook her head. 'Try again to free him,' she commanded, the old fierceness returning.

"'I've tried! It's not letting go!" The stain of blood was spreading through the snow.

"'Try harder!' She stood up and we both stamped on the side of the trap. All it did was make the jaws twist into General's leg. He panted with pain.

"'Bertie!' I yelled, and pushed her so hard she fell back into the snow. 'It's no good. The only way is to get the ax.'

"She squeezed her eyes shut, as if it were a nightmare she could wake up from. 'Stay here with him,' I said. 'I'll be back soon as I can.'

"'He's hurting so bad, Walt! We can't let him suffer.' I knew she couldn't stand to see him like this. Her eyes darted around the forest, twitchy and uncontrolled.

"'Bertie!' I spoke harshly and put the gun next to her. 'Stay with him. I'll be back soon as I can.'

"A crow flew over, cawing, and perched on a tree nearby. 'Damn bird,' I mumbled. Bertie trained her eyes on it.

"'It can smell the blood,' she whispered.

"'General's not gonna die. Not like this.' I had to get back to the farm quick. Every minute I waited, he'd lose more blood. His body was limp with pain. He didn't even turn his head to watch me go. Just as well. If he didn't make it till I got back, I didn't want the last thing he saw to be me leaving him.

"I ran through the snow as fast as I could, high-stepping it to break through the crust. I didn't want to think about what I had to do. The ax was resting against the woodpile beside the house. I grabbed it and found a sled for General. There were rags in the horse barn and I took some of them too. I piled everything onto the sled and took off back toward the forest.

"'Where you going?' Nigel called. He and Millard had been working on a snow fort all afternoon. I'd been hoping they wouldn't see me. I wasn't in the mood for their antics and I didn't want them telling Ma what had happened.

"I didn't trust myself to talk, so I ignored them, which only heightened their curiosity. They abandoned the fort and ran after me, crashing through the snow like two oxen.

"'Chopping firewood?' Nigel asked, catching sight of the ax. 'We still got lots. Anyhow, that's supposed to be my job now.'

"'You find a fishing spot?' Millard asked.

"'He's got no rods, dumb-dumb.'

"Lugging the sled behind me was going to make the trek back to General twice as long. I worried about him trying to gnaw at his leg to get free. I worried that Bertie wouldn't be able to stay calm and comfort him.

"I decided to tell them. 'General's got his leg caught in a trap.'

"The boys slowed for a second, and then picked up the pace to match mine. They didn't say anything, but Nigel took the rope out of my hands and started to pull the sled. 'How far in is he?'

"'Close to Bertie's shack.'

"Our breath came out in puffs of steam as we made our way into the forest. We couldn't walk three across, so I led and the twins followed behind.

"Then, from farther in, I heard a growl—and then the crack of the shotgun.

"My heart leapt to my throat. We picked up the pace, scrambling as fast as we could through the snow. 'Bertie!' I shouted.

"Bertie spun around at the sound of our approach. In her hands was the gun. At her feet lay General.

"A hundred emotions flooded me at once. What had I been thinking, leaving her with the gun? I stared at General. Had she shot him?

"I held up my hand to stop the boys. 'Bertie?' My voice cracked, the exertion and fear making it tremble. 'We heard a gunshot.'

"Bertie dropped the barrel of the gun into the snow. She looked too weak to hold it up anymore. General lay still, not even stirring at the sound of my voice.

"'The dogs,' her voice cracked. 'Two of them came right up to that tree.' She pointed to a tree not six feet from her. 'They were hunting.' General raised his head then and whimpered. The way he flopped back down, I could tell he was exhausted. The twins flanked me, watching Bertie carefully. They hadn't forgotten what she'd done to Herbie, and now that she'd grown stronger, some of their wariness had returned.

"'Is that why you fired?' I said.

"'I had to scare them away.' She came toward me and handed back the gun. A flush of shame rose up my neck. I didn't want to admit what I'd thought she'd done. I passed the gun to Millard and threw him a warning look not to be stupid with it. Nigel and I bent down to get a closer look at General's leg.

"Nigel's eyes strayed from the steel-jaw trap to the chain locked around the tree. I saw the pieces click together in his head. 'That's why you needed the ax,' he said quietly.

"'Yeah. No other way to get him free now.'

"Bertie's breath came in gulps. 'You could chop down the tree.'

"I swallowed. 'The tree's too big, Bert. Only way General's getting free is if I—' The words stuck in my throat. 'There's no other way.'

"Bertie's face contorted. She ran to the sled and grabbed the ax. 'No! You can't! You can't do that to him!'

"'He's been stuck in that thing for two hours already. He doesn't have much time left. We need to get him out right now. It'll be dark soon.You think I want to do this?' I fought back the tears choking me. 'Give me the ax.'

"'No!' She clutched it against her chest. I felt Nigel and Millard shift toward me, ready to back me up if need be.

"'Give it to him,' Millard said.

"Bertie looked at us, her eyes wild. She turned the blade of the ax in our direction. For a second—a split-second that felt like forever—I thought she was gonna take a swing at me.

"'There's no other way,' I said quietly. 'I'll do it quick, I promise. And then we'll take him home and bandage him up.'

"Bertie's breath came out in fast bursts.

"'You can go home, get a bed ready for him. The boys and I will bring him to you.'

"Bertie's chin quivered. Her eyes were brimming with tears.

"I took a step closer to her and held out my hand. 'Please, Bertie. He's suffering.'

"She squeezed her eyes shut and handed me the ax."

Mr. Pickering broke off, took a shaky breath, and started talking again. "I don't like thinking about what came next," he said. "I did what I had to do." His voice ached with the memory.

"We got General home and Ma bandaged him up best she could. Ma didn't say one word about letting a dog in the house, but he stayed by the fire for a week as he healed. Bertie slept on the floor beside him at night, the two of them curled up together under a quilt.

Mr. Pickering offered a rare smile. "I coaxed him to stand one day with a piece of rabbit meat that I dangled in front of him. That half leg was just a stump, but he could balance on the other three. I stood a few feet away and called to him. Bertie was right beside him. His first steps were clumsy, but once he got his balance, he made it to me. The twins cheered and even Ma clapped. We all needed some good news after that winter."

He stopped and took a shaky breath. It took everything in me not to beg Mr. Pickering to keep talking. But I could see he was worn out.

"Where are you going?" he asked when Harvey and I stood to go.

"I got my chores to do for Grandpa," I said.

"Will you come again?"

"Yeah, for sure. Tomorrow, probably."

"Oh, good," he said with a sigh.

I shook my head as I left his room. I wished I'd given Mr. Pickering a chance a long time ago.

Chapter 26

Maggie

It is Thursday, and there are still no leads to Harvey's where-abouts. Maggie's optimism is leaking out of her like a slow-ly deflating balloon. She keeps her eyes and ears open as she walks home. She reads online stories about amazing animal reunions. A dog—lost in the woods for three years—suddenly shows up at his owner's home. A cat that accidentally boards a plane and flies to South America is returned six months later.

She made new posters last night and added a line: $1,000 Reward for Safe Return. In her heart, there is no price she can put on Harvey, but $1,000 is all she has. Actually, she only had $982 saved up from birthday and Christmas, but Brianne and Lexi both put in nine dollars to help find Harvey. She has gone behind her parents' backs to have these signs made, and begged a teacher at school to photocopy fifty of them. Maggie thinks her parents will be angry that she's used her savings to find Harvey, but she doesn't care.

Maggie and her friends will go after school to put up the posters in other areas of the city. Brianne's mother has offered to take some to her work—a middle school across the city—and pin them up.

Chapter 27

Through the crowd of kids hanging around the entrance doors, I could see a Lost Dog poster. Mrs. Miller had just put it up on the community news bulletin board. The bell was about to ring, so I had to push my way forward to get a better look at it.

Please don't let it be Harvey.

But I knew it was him before I was close enough to read his name. In the photo, he was tilting his head as if he didn't understand a question. He'd been groomed, and his white fur was full and fluffy. LOST DOG was written in bold letters across the top. On the bottom, it said: $1,000 Reward.

His owner wanted him back. One thousand dollars. I could imagine what Mom would say if I came home with all that money. It would help. A lot.

But I'd have to give up Harvey.

My heart raced. I glanced around quickly. Mrs. Miller had gone back to her classroom. I waited for the bell to ring. As everyone jostled through the entrance doors, I ripped the poster off the board and jammed it into my backpack.

I had to think this through. If there was a poster at school, where else would it be hung up? At the rec center? The grocery store? What if there were Lost Dog posters all over the neighborhood? What if Mom saw a poster? Or Grandpa?

Instead of going to class, I turned around and went outside. My head was spinning as I ran back to my apartment. Grandpa wouldn't have picked Harvey up yet. I still didn't know what I was going to do when I put the key in the lock and heard Harvey bark on the other side of the door.

Chapter 28

Harvey

After Austin leaves for the morning, Harvey goes back to bed and waits for Phillip. This home is quiet—too quiet for Harvey's liking.

He jumps up when he hears the lock click. Ears pricked, he goes to investigate. He can smell Austin before he sees him. Austin's sweat and the cold of the outside have mixed together in a most pleasing way. What a wonderful surprise! He can't hold back a bark of greeting and is even more thrilled when he sees Austin grab the leash. He knows what that means! A walk! He jumps up and stretches against the boy's legs, but Austin steps away. Harvey notices his voice is different; his movements are jerky and sharp. Harvey's tail goes up, on high alert.

Harvey lets Austin clip the leash onto his collar. There is no elevator in the building, so Austin and Harvey race down the stairs to get to the main floor and fly through the front door. Harvey goes straight to his first stop, already coated with so many new smells. He lifts his leg to leave his own and then feels the tug on the leash. Austin is ready to run. There is no time for sniffing. Harvey's feet barely touch the ground as he races with Austin, the wind whistling past his ears.

Both of them breathless, they arrive at Brayside. Harvey pants and runs for the bowl of water behind the desk. His heart is thumping and he is invigorated. He circles back to Austin. The boy bends down. His voice is thick and his breath comes in bursts. Austin pulls Harvey against him and hugs him to his chest.

Harvey has a vague memory of being hugged this way before. Her hair used to tickle his nose, and he'd curl up on her bed in that cozy spot in the crook of her knees. He can almost hear the high-pitched cadence of her voice. A pang of loneliness hits Harvey. Raising his nose in the air, he tries to detect a whiff of her scent.

But of course, there is nothing.

Chapter 29

Austin

As soon as I got to Brayside, I called Grandpa. "You don't need to pick up Harvey," I told him. "There's no school today. Gas leak. They sent all the kids home." I curled my toes as the lie slid off my tongue. "We're here waiting for you."

My eyes ached from trying to hold back tears. I was doing the wrong thing, and I knew it. I should have dug the Lost Dog poster out of my backpack, called the number, let Harvey's owner know he was safe, and collected the reward.

But I wasn't ready to let Harvey go. Not just for me anymore. For Mr. Pickering too. He'd never said two words to me until Harvey showed up.

I knew it was selfish to keep Harvey now that I'd seen the poster. I went from being a good kid taking in a stray to a dog-napper, keeping Harvey from his owner.

"What are you doing here?" Mary Rose bent down to pat Harvey.

"No school today," I said.

"Well, it's probably good you showed up. I've got some bad news." She frowned, and my breath stuttered in my throat. "About Mr. Pickering."

I couldn't breathe, waiting for her spit it out.

"Is he—?" I couldn't bring myself to say the words. He looked better yesterday, even after telling the long story about General's leg. A hard knot burned in my chest. *I shouldn't have let him keep talking yesterday.*

"We're moving him to the second floor tomorrow."

"Moving." I sighed with relief. "Tomorrow?"

"We think it's for the best." I didn't listen to anything else Mary Rose said. I just took off down the hall with Harvey at my heels.

It wasn't Mr. Pickering who answered the door—this time it was Louise. Her dark skin glowed against the white of her uniform.

"Morning, Austin. What are you doing here?"

"No school," I said. I held Harvey back so he wouldn't go bounding in.

"Mr. Pickering," she said extra loud, even though there was nothing wrong with his hearing. "Look who's here! Austin!"

Then she turned to me and said quietly, "He says he's not hungry, but he didn't eat much dinner last night." She made a note on a clipboard and put it in the holder on the door. "I'll be back in an hour or so to check on him." A tray of food sat on the coffee table in front of him.

"Is he okay?" I asked.

Louise didn't nod right away. "You know he's being moved upstairs."

"Mary Rose told me."

"I don't think he's happy about it," she whispered. "And I can't believe I'm going to say this, but I'm not either."

"I know what you mean," I said.

"I know you do." Louise squeezed my arm and looked down at Harvey. "Harvey's going to miss him too, I bet." Harvey and I were welcome to go where we wanted on the first floor, but the second floor was different. I wasn't family and neither was Harvey. I didn't know the nurses as well up there. What if they didn't like us hanging around?

"I'll see you later, Mr. Pickering. You have a nice visit with Austin," Louise called, and shut the door once Harvey and I were inside the suite.

Mr. Pickering was in his recliner as usual. He twisted his head to look toward us when I let Harvey go.

"General," he mumbled.

"It's Harvey," I said. He jumped up on the recliner, and Mr. Pickering shifted over to give him space to lie down. He put a hand on his chest as if he were checking his heart. His eyes were watery.

"Austin," he sighed. "They're moving me upstairs."

"Yeah, I heard."

"Guess it's time," he said.

"The second floor's not so bad."

Mr. Pickering shot me a look, like he wasn't buying my BS. "I know what it's like. I know why they're moving me."

"I'll still come visit you," I said. *If I can.*

Mr. Pickering rested his head and stared at the tray of food Louise had left. He let out a long sigh.

"Did I ever tell you about the summer of 1936?" he asked. I shook my head.

He shifted in his chair and I settled in to listen.

"Nineteen thirty-six was the longest, hottest, and driest summer on record. Worse than all the other summers, which no one thought was possible. Bertie and I were thirteen that year, and we did what we could to keep the farm running. All the money that Pa had made in the bush over the winter had gone to pay off credit at Hackett's and to buy some vegetable seeds for Ma's garden. Our fields, like everyone else's, lay empty. I tell you, you'd have thought you were looking at the Sahara Desert, not the prairies.

"The only green things were in Ma's small plot of vegetables we were hoping to harvest come fall. I'd haul water from the pond, which had all but dried up, using two pails attached to a rod across my back. The twins said I looked like a mule, but I'd learned how to walk without spilling a drop. I think the two of them, Nigel especially, were jealous that Ma didn't trust them to help her. But we couldn't risk even one plant being trampled by their clumsy feet. My arms and legs had gotten stronger from all the work. Despite it being a drought, I wasn't looking like such a scrawny kid anymore.

"We kept some chickens, and still had our cows. Pa had started a business as a traveling mechanic, going to farms to fix tractors and the like. The farmers paid whatever they could offer, which usually wasn't much. Like everyone else, we were getting by on relief, delivered in train cars to the station in Weyburn once a month.

"This one day, me and Bertie were out watering Ma's garden when I stood up and saw something in the distance.

"'What's that?' I raised my arm and pointed at a cloud of dust on the blurred horizon. 'Is it a horse?' We stood watching as whatever it was moved closer. General ran out from the barn and panted beside me.

"We hadn't seen men on horseback in a while. People couldn't afford to keep a horse, except for plowing. And if they had one, they weren't galloping across the prairie like that, with nothing but a sea of sand in front of them. We saw mules. And carts loaded up with a family's possessions rolling past like a funeral procession. But not galloping horsemen.

"'There's three of them,' Bertie said, squinting. The horses moved in unison, their hooves kicking up a wall of dust.

"The twins came out of the house, followed by Ma with three-year-old Sylvia in her arms. I think she was worried they had news of Pa. I remember looking back at her and seeing the frown lines etched into her forehead, a few wisps of hair blowing against her face.

"Those were the days when sand got into everything. Even the food on your plate. Clothes that had been hidden in trunks had to be shaken out before you could wear them. Sometimes, after a real bad dust storm, the sand on the table was so thick we could write our names in it.

"'Who are they?' Bertie asked.

"'Bertie, Millard—take Sylvia inside,' Ma said, handing my sister over to Millard. 'Give her some milk and keep her quiet.'

"Millard started to argue. He didn't want to go inside. But he was the smallest of us boys. Ma shot him a look that said, *Just do it*. So he did.

"General was tense beside me, as if he didn't like the looks of the men either. His tail was up and his ears were pricked, as if he were trying to catch every sound in the air. His gait was different now. He hopped more than he ran. But even with three legs, he was the best darn farm dog we ever had.

"We could see the three men more clearly now. They were all the color of sand, covered head to toe in dust. They had pulled their handkerchiefs over their mouths and noses against the dust, but it made them look like bandits. General started to bark as soon as they came onto our property. I put my hand out to silence him.

"One of the riders pulled out front and reined his horse in, so it slowed to a canter as he passed our well. They didn't call to us, introduce themselves, or offer a greeting like you'd expect. They rode past Ma's garden, the barn, and the woodpile, looking around like they owned the place.

"Ma's expression got hard. She didn't move or say anything— just stared at the three interlopers. A bad feeling rose in my gut. Beside me, Bertie shifted and I heard her breath quicken.

"Pa had always warned us about desperate men. He said it was easy to underestimate what a desperate man might do. I figured he'd been around enough of them to know—and I tried to remember that as the three horsemen stared down at me. At the ripe old age of thirteen, I was the man of the house in my father's absence.

"'Afternoon,' one of them drawled as he pulled down his kerchief and tipped his hat. A line of dust was drawn across his face where the kerchief hadn't covered. The bottom half was unshaven. Even from where I stood, I could smell the stink of the road on them. Sweat, leather, and unwashed flesh made my eyes water. None of them got off his horse, which would have been the polite thing to do. I looked toward the road in hopes of seeing Pa and his cart trundling along. But the road was empty.

"'Can I help you?' Ma spoke up.

"'Well, yes. Yes, you can.' He turned to the other two. 'Didn't I tell you people 'round here were friendly?' They shot each other sidelong glances, and I watched as they took in the green of the garden plot and the tractor that Pa had taken out of the shed to tinker with earlier that day. We weren't thriving, but we'd make it through the summer. Pa would go into the bush as usual and come home with money to see us through another year.

"Normally, Ma would have offered guests a drink of water, or barley coffee. But with these three, she just stared as she waited to find out what they wanted.

"'A friend of ours told us about your place.'

"I narrowed my eyes. 'Who's that?' General growled beside me. He didn't like the looks of them either. The fact that they still hadn't dismounted to talk to us was an act of hostility.

"'A man we met up in Prince Albert. Told us there were some good people down this way who'd be more than happy to show us some hospitality. He mentioned a farm house just like this one.'

"I figured they were lying, but Bertie piped up. 'What's his name?'

"'Joe. Said he had a cabin 'round here too, tucked in the bush. Said we was welcome to stay there if we wanted.'

"'Joe what?'

"The man snorted. 'What's it to you?'

"Bertie narrowed her eyes and glared at them. I knew what she was thinking. We hadn't talked about her pa, or his absence, in a long time. It must have weighed on her, though, wondering where he was and if he was still alive.

"'When was this?' I asked, making my voice deeper than it was.

"The one at the back leaned down over his bridle. 'Couple weeks ago.' The leader shot him a look.

"'Is he still there?' Bertie asked.

"The front man stared at her and sucked on his teeth. They must have been as dry as chalk. I could hear the thickness in his voice. 'What do you care?'

"She shrugged. 'I'm curious 'bout why a man from 'round here would tell you three something like that. Unless he owed you.'

"One of them snorted. 'She's got it pretty well figured out.'

"Bertie pressed her lips together and jutted her chin forward. She muttered curses under her breath. Ma stiffened beside me, not because of Bertie's cursing, but because she'd also put two and two together. With no way to pay his debt, Bertie's good-for-nothing pa had sold us out. These men would take what they could from us to settle up with him. How many other farms had they ransacked today?

"General gave a low growl that came deep in his chest. At first, I thought he was growling at the men. But then I saw what it was that had drawn his attention. A dust storm was coming. Like a giant wall of sand, it was quickly rolling toward us.

"I took a step backward and glanced at Ma. She'd seen it too, and her eyes widened. 'Bertie, get inside. Walter and I will handle this.'

"The horses were getting antsy, shuffling from side to side as their owners issued subtle threats. A shotgun was attached to each man's saddle—plus a coil of rope, a sleeping roll, a blanket, and a canteen.

"'So what exactly can we do for you? My husband will be back soon. Maybe you should speak to him.'

"The three men laughed. 'No, you'll do just fine. We like this place. Looks like you got more than others around here.'

"My eyes were glued to the dust cloud. There's a moment before it hits when everything goes still and it feels like the air is getting sucked out of the sky. The dust on the ground rises slightly, as if it's levitating. Then the suffocating cloud rolls over.

"With their backs to the storm, the men must have thought the panic that showed on our faces was due to them. But all at once, all hell broke loose. General's growling turned into a ferocious bark. He leapt at the leader's horse, gnashing his teeth at the animal's legs.

"The front door of the house slammed open. Bertie stood there with the shotgun aimed at the leader's chest. Then the first swell of the cloud blew up around us, blinding me.

"Through the swirling cloud of dust, I saw General lunge at another horse. It wheeled and reared, almost throwing the rider off. Bertie fired the gun, and it went off with a blast, missing the men but scaring the horses.

"'Get inside!' Ma yelled. Dust filled our mouths and lungs. I coughed and pulled my shirt up over my face. Bertie had left the door open, and I grabbed onto the doorframe so I could stand up.

"'General!' I called, but my voice was torn away by the wind. I squinted in the direction of the horsemen. The horses were spinning about in confusion and didn't know which way to go. The riders shouted at their horses and each other.

"General—my three-legged attack dog—chased them into the dust cloud, barking like a blood-thirsty beast. I called for General again. But he didn't come.

"'Get inside!' Ma bellowed, and yanked me by the arm.

"I wouldn't go. I held on to the doorframe, searching for General. The dust storm blinded me. I couldn't see farther than the nose on my face.

"'General!' I hollered. I couldn't leave him outside, not with the bandits and their stamping horses' hooves. He could get caught underfoot and trampled, or buried in the mounds of sand deposited by the storm. Ma tugged on the door, battling the wind. Already the floor of our house was covered with drifts of sand, as if we were being overtaken by desert. But this wasn't the Sahara; it was the prairie.

"'Walt!' she screamed. 'Help me!'

"It took all our strength to pull the door closed. But even with the front door shut tight, dust came in under the door, through the cracks between the windows, and down the chimney.

"Sylvia was hollering and crying. The boys had her hidden under the bedcovers. Ma shoved me under the table beside Bertie, who had buried her face between her knees. I took the shotgun from her and clutched it against my chest, trying to protect it from the swirling grit.

"I crouched there, listening to General bark until he went silent. All I could do was pray that he'd be okay.

Chapter 30

Maggie

It is a half hour before dismissal when Maggie is called to the office. She knows it has to be something about Harvey. Her heart hammers in her chest. Is it bad news? For a minute, when she closes her classroom door behind her, she hesitates. If it were bad news, her mother would wait until she was home to tell her. So maybe, just maybe, it is good news. Maggie stands in the hall with balled fists. She squeezes her eyes shut, wishing with everything in her that Harvey has been found.

Maggie's mother is standing outside the office door. Maggie picks up her pace, resisting the urge to yell, "Did you find Harvey?" down the corridor.

Her mother isn't smiling, so Maggie knows she hasn't found him. Her shoulders sag.

Maggie's mother puts a hand on her shoulder and leans down so they are face to face. "I got a tip," she says. "A woman saw a Westie in a red harness. He was on Broadway."

"Broadway?" Maggie gapes at her mother. "That's downtown!"

"I know! But if it was him, we've been looking in the wrong places all this time."

"We have to go down there! Put up posters!"

Maggie's mother pulls a sheaf of them from her bag. "Get your things. I already signed you out. Dad is going to pick up the girls from daycare."

Tears well in Maggie's eyes, and she throws her arms around her mother. For the first time since Harvey's disappearance, Maggie feels hope. It spills out of her like an overflowing cup as she races to her locker to get her jacket.

Please, please, let us find him, she prays.

Chapter 31

Austin

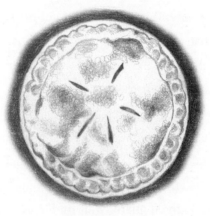

The way Mr. Pickering told it, even though the dust from that storm settled so long ago, I felt as if I were caught in it with Bertie and his family.

"The storm lasted all day and into the night. It was like a blizzard. We were trapped in the house. I worried about General. He could have been trampled by one of the horses, got lost in all the sand, or buried.

"Bertie kept saying he'd be okay. Animals seem to know how to keep safe. 'Probably found his way into the barn,' she said. The two of us were tucked under the table, holding wet rags over our mouths. Ma had Sylvia cradled in her arms, a blanket covering both of them. The twins lay under their bed, playing Xs and Os in the dust on the floor.

"'It was my pa,' she seethed, 'who sent them thieves.'

"Bertie was as loyal as General. I knew how much it hurt her to think bad of her pa, never mind say it out loud.

"I didn't know what those men had been planning to do to us. Rob us for sure. But what else? It got me shaking, thinking about what could've happened if the dust storm hadn't rolled through.

"'They might come back,' Bertie said quietly.

"I made a silent promise to myself that if there was a next time, I'd be ready. I swallowed back a lump of shame at how I'd failed to defend our home. I was man of the house, but it was Bertie who'd had the sense to get the gun. And it was General who'd caught them off guard. Wait till Pa heard that I'd stood by uselessly while a girl and a three-legged dog chased the men away.

"The morning after the storm, I had to climb out a window at the back of the house. The sand drift in front of the door was too high for me to open it.

"'General!" I shouted. I got nothing back but a mouthful of dirt. We'd had to conserve water by then. My first job of the day was to go to the well to fill the bucket.

"'General!' I called again. Bertie was behind me, doing the same.

"We saw no sign of the bandits. 'General!' Bertie hollered.

"The door to the barn creaked open, and a flurry of squawking chickens exploded out. We could hear the cows moo to be milked and fed.

"And then we heard a yelp.

"General ran out, looking none the worse for wear. He circled excitedly around Bertie, who laughed and pointed at me. 'Go see Walt!'

"I put the bucket down and got to my knees. General bounded over to me and licked my face. He probably got a mouthful of dust too. I put some water in my hands and let him lap it up. Then he went back to racing between me and Bertie.

"Later that day, we swept sand out of the barn by the shovelful. Bertie stopped working and said, 'I hate him, Walt.' The thought of her pa had probably been gnawing on her all day. 'Not like I hate Herbie Caldwell, or leeches—but in this other way.' She broke off and shook her head. 'It's like I'm frozen with it. It scares me sometimes. I think I could kill him.'

"I looked at her. The days were long and the sun hadn't set yet. The sky was dusky purple through the open barn door.

"'If he's in Prince Albert, that's only a few hours away. There's no reason he couldn't send for me, or come back to make sure I was okay.' Bertie shook her head. 'He left me to starve or freeze to death. What kind of a man does that? He's supposed to be my father, look after me. I hope he rots in hell.'

"'Bertie,' I started, thinking I could say something to ease her mind. She gave me a hard look, her chin jutted forward and her eyes narrowed. I kept quiet. Bertie wasn't one to say anything she didn't mean.

"Pa came home later that evening. A cloud of dust billowed up behind him as he drove the horse into our yard. The twins blurted about the bandits before he'd even stepped down from the wagon.

"'General scared them off,' Nigel said. 'Bit one of the horses!'

"Pa looked at General and raised an eyebrow. If he'd been home when the dog lost his leg, Pa probably would have shot General.

"'No kidding.'

"'And Bertie got the gun!' The twins mimicked her shooting at the bandits. Millard pretended to be shot as he clutched his chest and fell to his knees in a death scene. Pa looked at me. I lowered my head. I didn't want to tell him that I'd just stood there while Bertie'd had the sense to defend our home."

All of sudden, Mr. Pickering stopped. He took a gaspy breath. I rose half out of my seat. "Mr. Pickering?"

But then he took a deeper breath. It rattled through his chest, and he closed his eyes.

"I'll get a nurse," I said, and started for the door.

"No," he said. "Not yet. Please."

I hesitated.

"I have more to tell you. About Bertie." He took another breath, a little easier this time. "And General."

"You don't look so good, Mr. Pickering."

"I'm fine."

His eyes were still closed, so I thought maybe he just needed a rest. I waited, watching him anxiously.

"Sit down." Mr. Pickering's voice was steady. "I want to finish."

I swallowed my doubts, but I did what he said. It took him a few minutes to pull himself together. The whole time I was ready to spring up and call for the nurse. I stared at him, willing the color to come back into his cheeks. When he finally started talking again, his voice was quiet. I had to lean in close to hear him.

"We lived on edge for a couple of weeks. One day, Mr. Hackett said that three men had been caught trying to rob another homestead close to Prince Albert.

"There weren't many of us left on farms by the end of the summer. It seemed that every day another family decided they'd had enough and packed up what little they had and made for somewhere else. A few headed farther west. Some moved to the cities.

"Pa made plans to head into the bush for another season with the lumber company. I didn't want him to go, but I knew his wages were keeping our family afloat. By an unspoken agreement, Bertie stayed on with us. She helped Ma with Sylvia and the other chores around the house. I think Ma liked having the company, especially with my pa gone so much and me and the twins out of the house all day, looking after the animals or hunting.

"I'd become a better shot and took to bringing the gun with me whenever I left the house. General and I would roam over a wider and wider territory, looking for game. I knew Bertie wanted to come too. But as she got older, Ma didn't think it was proper for a girl to be out in the woods. I think she worried that some of Bertie's wildness would come back if she was left to her own devices. Keeping her safe on the farm had domesticated her. She could bake a pie now almost as well as Ma. She often made dinner for all of us.

"Pa was working on a neighbor's tractor. Ma had taken Sylvia and the twins to town with her. It was the boys' birthday and they'd each gotten fifty cents to pick out something at Hackett's. I'd teased them that if they weren't twins, someone would have gotten a whole dollar.

"I was cleaning out the chicken coop, and the smell of ammonia from their droppings was making me see double. I had to use Pa's rubber boots now that I'd outgrown mine—they were still too big on me and my feet swam in them as I clunked around the mud-packed floor.

"Bertie came out to find me. General had followed her and stood just outside the coop. Bertie stood in the doorway, hands in the pockets of her apron. Her red hair had darkened to auburn. She still kept it short; it hit the bottom of her earlobes. Her bare neck stuck out of the collar of her dress. She'd gained weight since she'd come to live with us, but it didn't seem to stick anywhere in particular on account of her shooting up. She was almost as tall as I was.

"'You gonna do this all day?' she asked, sitting down on a bucket.

"'Hope not.'

"'Wanna go hunting?' she asked hopefully.

"'I was thinking about it.'

"'Let's go now before it gets too hot. You can clean this out anytime.' I didn't need to be asked twice.

"As we left the stink of the chicken coop behind, General ran after us, excited that we were moving again. In the house, I grabbed a hunting knife and a canteen of water, and slung the shotgun around my neck. Bertie came out of the bedroom wearing a pair of the twins' old pants, patched a few times over the knees. She put a coil of rope over her head so it hung off one side like a cowboy's lasso. A slingshot hung out of one pocket. With her short hair and freckled face, she didn't look like a girl; she didn't look like a boy either. She looked like herself. I felt a flush of admiration for her—and maybe a bit of jealousy too.

"'What?' she asked.

"'Nothing,' I said, and whistled for General. We were a ragtag hunting party—that was for sure. But the day stretched out in front of us with promise. It had been a long time since the three of us went out together. Too long.

"Soon as we left our property line, the wind picked up. Bertie and I had to shield our eyes from the itching, stinging flecks of sand that blew into them. The smart thing to do would have been to turn back. A dust storm could rise up at any minute, and I stole glances at the horizon, half-expecting to see one billowing up. But neither of us spoke up.

"Soon as we got into the bush, the trees protected us. They were dry and brittle; the air crackled. It was impossible to walk silently. My foot snapped something everywhere I stepped—a leaf, a twig, a branch. No animal would be surprised by our approach. Bertie was in the lead, with General close behind, and me bringing up the rear. The butt of the shotgun knocked against the back of my thigh. I wasn't paying attention to where Bertie was leading me till it was too late.

"'What are we doing here?' I asked her. It had been months since I'd last seen her shack, and time hadn't been kind to it. The roof had collapsed, probably under the weight of the snow from the past winter. The walls sagged like they were too tired to stay upright. I sniffed the air, curling my lip at the stink that surrounded us.

"'Some kind of dead animal,' I muttered.

"We pulled our shirts up over our noses and went to investigate. The drought had left the bush quiet—birds kept to the shade and there weren't any mosquitoes, just lightning-fast flies. General's tail went down as we moved closer to the shack. He was antsy, coiling himself around our legs. He didn't like it there any more than we did. It dawned on me that maybe it wasn't a dead animal making that stink. Maybe it was something else.

"Bertie had probably already had that same thought, but I grabbed her arm anyway. I didn't want to go any farther. 'Let's go back,' I muttered.

"She looked at me, her eyes steely. 'I gotta see.' She shook her arm free and walked to the window. I hesitated for a second, then followed. There were just a couple of shards of glass left in the panes, and the smell got stronger as we drew closer. My stomach heaved and I had to fight back the vomit rising in my gut. I'd smelled plenty of dead things by then, but nothing like this.

"I stood beside Bertie, and we both peered through the window. A man was stretched out on the bed, half-tied boots still on. There was no doubt he was dead. His mouth hung open and his face was sunken. Where the eyes should have been, there were empty sockets. I imagined a crow sitting on his forehead poking its beak into a juicy eyeball.

"Bottles lay on the floor, some upright, some fallen over— all drained of whatever drink they had contained.

"'It's him, isn't it?' I asked.

"Bertie nodded. She gagged, then threw up against the side of the shack. I knew she'd wished him dead. But actually seeing him like that, well, no one would be prepared for such a thing. No one.

"'I'm sorry, Bert,' I said, which I guess I was. Sorry for her, anyway. For knowing how her pa had died, alone in a shack. Bertie had been at our place, a short walk away. It would have been nothing for him to look for her. But he hadn't bothered. Maybe he just didn't care.

"She held up her hand, a signal for me to stop the condolences. She took a swig of her water and spit it out. 'He deserved what he got.' She looked at me, dry-eyed. 'We should burn the place down.'

"I wasn't sure she was thinking straight. 'It's too dry. The whole thicket would go up.'

"She fixed me with one of her dark looks. 'I can't know he's here.'

"'We'll tell someone,' I suggested. "My pa, or Reggie. They'll know what to do. We can bury him proper, if that's what you want.'

"She spat. 'That's not what I want. I want him *gone*. He up and left me, no word for months! I'd be dead too, if it hadn't been for you and your ma. Last thing he deserves is a Christian burial.'

"I'd been to a few funerals by that time, and I knew that burials were for the people still living more than the people who'd died. There's some type of ending that happens when a coffin shuts. Bertie needed that, same as anyone. She had to say her piece to her pa, or she'd live with it forever.

"I grabbed her elbow and held on when she tried to shy away from me. 'What are you doing?' she growled.

"'Come on,' I said, dragging her toward the door.

"'Let go of me!' She swatted at me with her free arm. Her shout sent birds fluttering from the bushes. General whined.

"I stopped and looked at her. 'You got to let go of him. All the bad feelings stewing inside of you, they're gonna get worse unless you let them out.'

"She stopped struggling. 'I can't go in there.'

"'I'll be right beside you,' I said, and nudged the door open with my shoe. It creaked and banged against the wall. The smell was even worse inside—like rotting, putrid sludge. We were close enough to his body that I could see the maggots writhing on his skin, feasting.

"'Tell him. Tell him everything you want to say.' Bertie stood there, mute. 'Okay, I'll start.' I faced her pa. "You're a worthless human being. You never deserved a daughter as strong and smart and fearless as the one you got. Maybe it was all your carousing ways that made her so brave. But you lived like a coward and you died like one too. Bertie's right. This is what you deserve.' Hearing the words come out of my mouth, I knew they were the right ones to say. I turned to Bertie.

"She blinked and didn't say anything at first—just stared at what was left of her father. For a second, I thought she wasn't going to say anything. The defiant Bertie had drifted away. In her place was a scared, sad girl who wouldn't be able to shake this image of her pa for as long as she lived.

"*I shouldn't have dragged her in here*, I thought.

"When she finally spoke, her words were thick and raspy and not what I expected. They came from somewhere deep inside of her. 'I would have loved you.' She stared at him for another few seconds, then tore out of the shack like it was on fire.

"General had had the sense to stay outside. As soon as Bertie took off, he bounded through the brush beside her.

"'Bertie!' I shouted. 'Come back!' I had half a mind to let her run; she had General with her to keep her safe. She'd find her way home when she was ready.

"In the end, I did go after her. Couldn't bear the thought of going back to the farm by myself, not knowing where she was. I chased her and General through the bush, their shapes darting back and forth across my line of vision. Branches and sticks poked and jabbed me, scratching my face. With all my trappings, I was slower than she was. It wasn't long before I lost sight of her and General.

"Then a scream pierced the air.

"'Bertie!' I shouted. 'You okay?'

"There was a ferocious growl. I stopped where I was, listening.

"General's bark reminded me of the day the bandits had shown up. It gave me chills. I ran closer, pulling the shotgun around and holding it against my chest.

"'Get away!' Bertie shouted. A branch scratched me across the cheek and drew blood. I flinched at the sting of it and crouched low, trying to see through the underbrush. I spotted Bertie standing a little farther ahead, waving a branch in front of her. General's bark was loud, constant, and desperate.

"Three mangy dogs fanned out in front of Bertie. They looked half starved, which I knew made them even more dangerous. In response to a silent signal, they all took a step closer. Bertie backed up closer to me and waved the branch at their snouts. If she lunged too close, one could snap its jaws around her arm and haul her down. General, as strong as he was, was no match for the three of them.

"My fingers trembled as I held the gun in front of me. Sweat dripped into my eyes. I couldn't steady the shotgun on my shoulder—it kept slipping. Couldn't get a clear shot of the dogs either—I was afraid I could hit Bertie or General. I aimed the gun up to the sky and fired a warning shot. The dogs backed away, but didn't run. They were too desperate to be scared.

"My fingers fumbled as I dug a bullet out of my pocket and reloaded the shotgun. It slipped from my fingers onto the tinder-dry leaves on the ground. I glanced up from the gun. The dogs were moving closer.

"'Get away!' Bertie shouted again and stomped on the ground. She had backed up until she was against a tree with nowhere else to go. I got another bullet in and adjusted the rifle on my shoulder. I trained my sights on the middle dog.

"My finger was on the trigger when one of the dogs snarled and dove for General. The other two advanced on Bertie. She kicked and whacked at them with the branch. Now I couldn't risk shooting Bertie.

"'Bertie!' I shouted. I was about to fire another warning shot when suddenly General twisted away from his attacker. He threw himself in front of Bertie. All three dogs turned away from Bertie and went after General.

"Bertie shrieked, beating at them with her stick. With a battle cry, I held out the butt of the gun and charged, swinging at the dogs. General was on his side, struggling to stand. The dogs could taste blood. They went after General, greedily tearing into his flesh. The sound of their yelps and bloodthirsty growls made me frantic.

"'No!' I hammered at the dogs with the butt of the shotgun like a man possessed. I kicked and slammed them, catching one in the head. Another's legs buckled and he limped off into the bush. Bertie whacked one across the middle and he whimpered and backed away.

"Bertie and I stood, muscles tensed. We looked around the thicket, nerves taut, as we prepared for another attack. But the last dog turned and ran. Soon we heard the dogs bark from a distance. They'd left, for now.

"General lay at my feet. I dropped to my knees. His exposed side was a bloody, pulpy mess. His fur was torn away and his innards were exposed. His breath came in short gasps.

"'No, no, no!' Bertie cried, and went down on shaky legs beside him. We watched helplessly as his blood seeped into the ground.

"'General,' I choked out. He wasn't going to last long. I stroked his head, rubbing between his ears. Bertie ran her hand gently up and down his back.

"The dogs had ripped him apart. My heart broke to watch him suffer.

"And then I knew I'd have to finish what they hadn't.

"I didn't want to do it. But I had to. I wanted to make General better. I wanted him to know how much I loved him.

"Bertie knew what I was thinking. 'You have to do it,' she whispered. 'He's hurting.'

"'I'm sorry,' I said. Tears filled my eyes and rolled down my cheeks. I put my lips against his fur and inhaled his scent, filling my body with one last breath of him.

"Bertie and I stood. 'Back up,' I said, and held the butt of the gun against my shoulder. Killing deer, rabbits, and squirrels is nothing like killing something you love. The pull of the trigger took an eternity. When the hammer came down at last, a flock of birds exploded into the sky.

"His body jolted once, and then he lay still.

"Bertie and I sat beside General all afternoon. I didn't want the dogs to come back to take away another piece of him. Neither of us said a word. I was sick of it all—death and suffering, seeing people I loved get hurt. Anger filled me. I didn't know how to get rid of it.

"Finally, Bertie stood. General was gone. His body was stiff—like every other dead thing I'd seen in my thirteen years. Like Bertie's pa. Like I would be one day too.

"It hit me then, how useless all of it is. The fighting against something that's gonna happen no matter what.

"'I'm sorry.' Bertie's voice was thick. 'I'm sorry for everything.'

"'Wasn't your fault,' I said, but I couldn't look at her.

"'It was.' She turned and started walking back home. I bent down and rested my head on General's. I wanted to hug him one more time, feel his warmth against my chest, and let him know he meant the world to me. But his scent was gone. Already his body was starting to rot in the heat.

"'Goodbye,' I murmured."

Mr. Pickering stopped and sighed.

I knew this had happened more than eighty years ago. I knew General would be long gone now anyway. But my eyes burned with tears. I didn't want General to be dead.

"Things weren't the same between me and Bertie after that. It wasn't just her. I changed too. Couldn't stand the thought of being around the farm without General. School felt like a place for little kids now, so I stopped going. I guess I moved into myself, sort of. I shrank away from the rest of the world.

"It was my idea to go into the bush with Pa that fall. There was nothing left for me on the farm, and Nigel and Millard were old enough to look after things. Pa agreed, knowing I'd make good money with him. The twins weren't sad to see me go, but I expect my ma was—though she didn't say it. Bertie didn't come outside to see me off. She was sore at me for leaving her, so we never said a proper goodbye.

"I sent letters home. Ma wrote to tell me Bertie'd taken to sleeping in the barn, like I used to. Ma didn't think it was right for a girl to sleep out there, but she couldn't chain Bertie up in the house either.

"By the time I came home with Pa in the spring, Bertie had gone. She'd left one day with a change of clothes and a bit of food. Ma was beside herself. She had Reggie and Mr. Hackett and everyone else she could think of look for Bertie. But it was like she'd disappeared into thin air."

Mr. Pickering's hand went to his chest again. I wiped away the tears that I couldn't hold back anymore. "You found her, though, right?"

Mr. Pickering shook his head. "Never heard from her again. Never knew what happened to her till I read her obituary in the paper." His eyes fell on a shiny wooden box on the coffee table. "I cut it out and saved it. You can read it if you like."

There was a knock at the door, and Harvey let out a half-hearted *woof*. But he didn't seem interested in leaving his spot on the recliner.

"You should get it." Mr. Pickering said to me. "It might be Ma."

Mary Rose was at the door. Harvey jumped down from the recliner and came over to greet her.

"You crying?" she asked, peering into my face.

"We were talking about his dog, General—"

"Ma? Is that you?" Mr. Pickering called from his chair.

Mary Rose looked at me, her eyes beetle-black and narrowed.

"Mr. Pickering, it's Mary Rose." She bustled past me and into the room. "Feeling okay, Mr. Pickering?" she asked him.

"Why wouldn't I be?" Mr. Pickering looked at her like she was an intruder. It reminded me of the man I used to think he was—a grumpy old guy who hated everyone. Mary Rose didn't answer, but scolded me with her eyes.

Harvey left my side and headed back to the recliner, putting his paws up on Mr. Pickering's lap. With a trembling hand, the old man reached down to rub the spot between Harvey's ears.

"I should have gone looking for Bertie," he said. He stared at me. "But Ma always said she was a wild thing. So I let her go."

"What's he talking about?" Mary Rose whispered.

"His best friend when he was a kid." My voice was thick.

"I never should have let her go," he mumbled. Then his head was in his hands and he sobbed quietly.

I couldn't just let Mr. Pickering sit there crying, so I went to his recliner and crouched down beside it. I held his hand. It was knotted with veins, the skin loose and translucent.

"There was nothing you could have done," I said. "It was a long time ago. Bertie would have forgiven you."

"Do you think so?" he asked.

"Yeah. She would have. I know it." That seemed to give him some peace. He rested his head back against the chair and closed his eyes, but he didn't let go of my hand. A minute later he was breathing heavily.

"Austin?" Mary Rose murmured. "What's going on?"

It was hard to put it all into words. I could feel the gears in my brain grinding slowly as I searched for a way to explain it all to Mary Rose. Finally, I said, "He's trying to let go."

Mary Rose put a hand on my shoulder. "You want to stay with him till he wakes up?" she asked.

"Sure," I said, and gently pulled my fingers out of Mr. Pickering's grip. He stirred a little.

"Goodbye, Bertie," he said in his sleep.

Chapter 32

Harvey can't settle. He has tried to find the spot beside Mr. Pickering that he usually lies in, but it doesn't feel right. The old man's body is tense, as if he's waiting for something.

Harvey is on edge. He knows he must stay close, alert for whatever danger is coming.

Harvey tries to get Austin's attention. He nudges the boy's leg with his nose as if to say, *Can't you feel it?*

Mr. Pickering's scent is fading. His heart is weakening, each beat fainter than the last. Harvey stares at Austin, willing him to understand.

"What is it, Harvey?" Austin asks.

Of course, Harvey can't explain what he senses is coming for the old man. But if he could, the fate of our story and the lives of Austin, Mr. Pickering, and Maggie would take a very different turn.

Chapter 33
Austin

Harvey kept sniffing around the recliner, jumping up and then back down. He stared at me with his head tilted, as if he were trying to tell me something.

Mr. Pickering slipped in and out of sleep, until he finally jolted upright, fully awake. He looked so confused, I braced myself for the awkwardness of explaining who I was again. But then his face changed.

"They're moving me upstairs, aren't they?" Mr. Pickering said.

I nodded.

Mr. Pickering sighed. He looked frail. "When?"

"Soon, probably. Your heart—"

Mr. Pickering waved a hand and snorted. "My heart." His voice caught, as if he were going to cry. I was still sitting on the floor by his chair where Mary Rose left me. I wished I could do something.

"Austin," he said, "I'd like to go for a walk."

I thought he meant down the hallway, so I nodded. That was good news, right? I figured that if he had enough energy to leave his suite, maybe he wasn't feeling as bad as I thought.

"Okay!" I said, and stood up, ready to help him out of the recliner.

But then he threw me for a loop by saying, "Outside."

"Outside," I repeated.

"Yes. Outside."

As soon as Harvey heard the word "outside," he raced to the door and started pawing it.

"When they ship me up to the second floor, that could be it," Mr. Pickering said gruffly. "I'd like to breathe fresh air one more time."

"I don't know, Mr. Pickering," I said.

"You can bundle me up in a wheelchair. Other people go out for walks. We don't need to go far." He staggered out of the recliner and I reached out to grab him. His weight on my arm felt solid.

As soon as I opened the door, Harvey shot out and raced to the front desk, where we kept his leash. Mr. Pickering shuffled beside me.

"Good to see you up and about, Mr. Pickering," Mary Rose said, but she shot me a look that said, *Have you lost your mind?*

"We're taking Harvey out."

"Now?" Mary Rose asked. It was late afternoon and already getting dark.

"Spent my whole life outside," Mr. Pickering growled. "Sure as heck not going to let this place tell me what I can and can't do." I almost laughed to hear Mr. Pickering's crankiness return.

Mary Rose didn't look too sold on the plan, but at last she said, "Then I guess we're all going." She went back to his suite and dug out a winter jacket. When she brought it to him, I could see a layer of dust on the shoulders from hanging in the closet for so long. We set him up in a wheelchair and piled blankets on top, tucking them around his legs to keep him warm.

I didn't think he liked all the fuss. He stared straight ahead, his lips pressed tight together till we were done. Then Mary Rose and I put on our jackets. Harvey was circling like crazy, excited by all the activity and the promise of outside. Finally, I was ready to push Mr. Pickering's wheelchair through the sliding-glass doors and into the chilly November afternoon.

"Not too far," Mary Rose reminded me as we started down the street. I leaned over to check on Mr. Pickering. He was so loaded up with blankets that only his nose and mouth peeked out.

Harvey dragged Mary Rose to the first tree we came to and lifted his leg. But before he could pee, he put his leg down again. He froze and sniffed the air.

Mary Rose shook her head. "I guess he's picked up the scent of something." She yanked on the leash. "Come on, Harvey."

But Harvey wouldn't budge.

Chapter 34

Maggie

Maggie and her mother find a parking spot on Broadway, a terrific feat for the middle of a work day. The sidewalks are clogged with people, and at first Maggie is too timid to shout out Harvey's name.

But after a couple of hours, she no longer cares. Her voice rings out in a stretched-out two syllable call that echoes in her head as she walks.

"Harrr-veee!"

When she hears the first bark, it is so faint that she wonders if she has imagined it. But then it comes again, barely audible over the street noise.

You might think it would be impossible to tell one dog's bark from another's, but I bet you are able to pick out your mother's call in a crowded room. Harvey's bark has been embedded in Maggie's brain. She is sure it is him.

"Mom!" she whispers, clutching her mother's sleeve. *"Listen."*

Three more short barks.

"It sounds like Harvey!" Maggie cries.

They pick up the pace and head in the direction the barks come from, calling for Harvey.

Chapter 35

Austin

I couldn't tell what had spooked Harvey. He sniffed the air as
if his life depended on it. His tail stuck straight up. His ears
were pricked. He barked and barked, as if he were calling to
someone. Finally, we got him moving again.

We headed straight down Broadway. "How are you doing?"
I asked Mr. Pickering.

"Where's the dog? he said.

"He's right there with Mary Rose." I turned the wheelchair
a little so he could see Harvey pulling on his leash.

"Not that one. General. Where is he?"

I groped for an answer. "He—he's not here."

Mr. Pickering looked up at me, panic stricken.

I needed to say something to soften the blow. "He was a really great dog, though, wasn't he?"

Mr. Pickering's eyes were teary. I couldn't tell if it was from the cold or his memories of General. I figured it was time to go back to Brayside. But Harvey kept barking and tangling himself in our legs.

"Harvey!" Mary Rose said sharply. "What in the world is wrong?" She turned to me. Harvey was still in the middle of the sidewalk. He refused to move, even with Mary Rose tugging hard on his leash.

Then I turned to check on Mr. Pickering. He was slumped over in his chair. My guts turned ice cold. There was something about the way he was leaning forward with his head dropped to the side. It didn't look like he was asleep.

"Mary Rose!" I shouted. "Help!" She dropped Harvey's leash and was beside me in a heartbeat.

A second later, from the corner of my eye, I saw Harvey racing away.

Chapter 36
Harvey

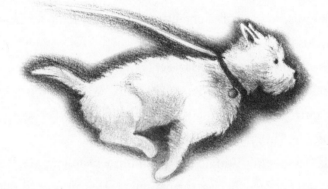

Maggie's scent wafts up Harvey's nose again. Every hair on his body bristles. He can feel Mary Rose tug on his leash, but he steels his legs and refuses to move.

He ignores Austin's call as he holds onto the scent. But then the boy's voice changes. The high-pitched, panicked shout raises Harvey's hackles. He feels the tension slacken as Mary Rose drops his leash and rushes to Mr. Pickering.

Harvey could go now. Free from Mary Rose's hold on his leash, he could run. He could follow his Maggie's scent. He could find her.

But he doesn't.

Austin shouts. Harvey knows that the commotion around Mr. Pickering means there is trouble. Just as he would alert his pack if he had one, Harvey tears down the sidewalk. He streaks across streets, dodging peoples' legs. What took almost half an hour—with all the starts and stops—takes Harvey only a few minutes. When he arrives at Brayside's front doors, he stands outside and barks. The noise echoes off the glass doors and brick walls, so instead of one little white dog calling for help, it sounds like many.

The doors glide open. "Harvey?" Phillip says. He steps onto the sidewalk and looks around for Austin. "What are you—"

"Come!" Harvey's yip says. He knows he has to get back to his people. They need him. Austin needs him.

Harvey doesn't wait to see if Phillip will follow. He just takes off. His legs fly over the pavement. He can hear Phillip puffing behind him and the jangle of his keys as he struggles to keep up.

Harvey races back to the old man. He smells his Maggie again. Her scent is strong, and he knows she must be nearby. He wants to stop and howl for her, let her know he is here. But dogs operate on instinct. Harvey's instinct tells him to deliver Phillip to Mr. Pickering. As much as he wants to, he can't stop for Maggie.

Chapter 37

Maggie

Maggie shouts for Harvey. Her voice is raspy now. She pauses at alleys and doorways, looking inside. Across the street, people are crowded around something. She can't see what it is. Parked cars block her view.

"Harrr-veee!" she shouts.

She hasn't heard him bark again. *Maybe I did imagine it,* she thinks with a heavy heart.

Nearby sirens blare. Across the street, Maggie sees a man running. In front of him is a blur of white.

"Harvey!" Maggie's heart jumps to her throat. "Harvey!"

Maggie's mother grabs her daughter's jacket before she

rushes blindly into traffic. Maggie points to the other side of the street.

"It's him! Right there! He's running with that man!" Maggie's face is alight with excitement. Tears overflow her eyes. "I saw him!" It was only a glimpse, a flash of white. But Maggie knows.

It *has* to be Harvey.

Chapter 38

Austin

I stood helplessly beside Mr. Pickering as Mary Rose told me
what to do. She had a 911 operator on the phone with her.

"Watch for the ambulance," she said to me. "Wave them
down so they know where we are."

I was too scared to ask if he was alive, but I heard her tell
the operator that his pulse was weak, so I knew he must be.
All I could think about was that it was my fault if something
happened to Mr. Pickering. He never would have been outside
if it hadn't been for me.

"Austin!" Grandpa shouted. I didn't know how Grandpa figured out where we were, and I didn't care. I was just glad he
was there.

I could hear the sirens now. I ran into the middle of the street and waved my hands over my head as if I were flagging down an airplane. An ambulance pulled over. I stumbled out of the way and stood beside Grandpa.

"How did you know?" I asked. The paramedics pulled the layers of blankets off Mr. Pickering and lifted him out of the wheelchair and onto a gurney.

"Harvey showed up at Brayside. The way he was acting, I knew something had to be wrong."

"Where is he?" I looked around, worried.

That's when I heard a girl laughing.

"Well, I'll be," Grandpa muttered. Behind us, sitting on the sidewalk was a red-haired girl, about twelve. Harvey was jumping up and down with excitement and covering her face with kisses. In the same instant, Grandpa and I both knew. Harvey had found his owner.

I moved away from Grandpa and walked over to Mr. Pickering. The paramedics were trying to keep him alert, but he was slipping in and out of consciousness.

"It's me, Mr. Pickering," I said. "Austin."

"Bertie," he whispered.

"No, sir. Austin." But then I saw that he wasn't looking at me. He was staring at the red-haired girl.

Mr. Pickering smiled. "They're waiting for me," he murmured, "so we can walk to Shell Creek."

His eyes flared bright like a candle for a second, and then slowly burned out. His lids drooped.

He took one last breath that shuddered through him. And then he was peaceful.

Chapter 39

Maggie

Maggie clutches Harvey to her chest and digs her fingers into his fur. She is so focused on Harvey that she is oblivious to events going on around her. She doesn't notice the man in blue coveralls approach her mother. She doesn't notice that the boy with him is wiping away tears.

"Maggie," her mother calls a few minutes later. "Come here." Reluctantly, Maggie stands up, cradling Harvey in her arms. "This is Phillip and his grandson, Austin. They found Harvey."

"He showed up outside of Brayside last week," says the man. "Austin took him in."

"Brayside?" Maggie's mother asks. "The retirement home?"

Phillip nods. The boy looks at Maggie from under a shaggy fringe. She narrows her eyes at him. He doesn't look like a dog thief, but she knows he must be. All he had to do was bring her dog to a vet or shelter, and they would have used the chip implanted in Harvey's neck to find his home.

"We're going to miss him," Phillip says. "He's become a fixture around Brayside. The residents love him."

"I'm sorry I kept him," Austin says. His voice is deeper than Maggie expected—hoarser. But then she realizes it's because he's holding back tears. "Do you think I could say goodbye to him? Before you leave?"

Maggie is tempted to say no—she really is. But Harvey is wiggling around in her arms, making it impossible to hold on to him. She puts him down on the sidewalk and keeps a firm grip on his leash as he darts to the boy.

Austin crouches down and holds Harvey's face in his hands. He whispers something she can't hear and then rubs the ruff around his neck. She always thought of Harvey as her dog, but seeing them together makes her realize that part of Harvey might belong to Austin too. The thought gives her a sharp pang.

Maggie bends down so she and Austin are eye level and only a few feet apart. Harvey licks Austin's hand and returns to Maggie.

"He's a really good dog," Austin says. His words are filled with emotion and almost unintelligible. Despite the odds,

Maggie has found Harvey and he is going home with her. Some of the bitterness she feels for Austin drains away.

"Thanks for looking after him." It's the most generous thing she can think of to say, considering the circumstances.

Austin's cheeks flush—with guilt, she thinks. Or maybe it's just that he is going to miss Harvey. She feels a rush of pity for him. She knows, just as well as he does, that dogs like Harvey are rare. Maybe one in a million.

"Austin," his grandpa calls. "We should go back."

Reluctantly, Austin stands up. "I help at Brayside after school every day, if you want to visit." The offer is halfhearted, as if he already knows what her answer will be.

But Maggie surprises both of them by saying, "Yeah. Maybe."

She knows how hard it was to lose Harvey for a week. She can't imagine losing Harvey for a lifetime.

Chapter 40

Austin

After the ambulance left, and Maggie and her mother took Harvey, Grandpa and I walked back to Brayside. Mary Rose had gone ahead to let everyone know what happened. Watching her leave with the empty wheelchair made it hard to swallow.

"He's in Heaven, right?" I asked Grandpa. It sounded like something a little kid might say, and I would have been embarrassed to ask anyone else.

"I like to think so."

"Me too." I wiped the tears off my cheeks.

"He lived a good life," Grandpa said. "You were lucky you got to hear about it."

"It was because of Harvey," I said. "He got Mr. Pickering talking."

Grandpa shook his head. "I think it was you, Austin. No point in talking if no one is there to listen."

When we got back to Brayside, Mr. Santos, Mr. Singh, Miss Lin, Mrs. Luzzi, and Mrs. O'Brien were waiting for me. Mary Rose, Louise, and Artie were there too. But it was Mrs. O'Brien who held out her arms and let me quietly sob against her shoulder.

"I know, Austin," she whispered. "I know."

I let Grandpa handle the explaining, and when I was ready, I went to Mr. Pickering's room. I raised my hand to knock on the door. When I realized I didn't have to, because no one was there to answer, the ache in my chest grew.

His suite was just how he'd left it. The lunch tray Mary Rose had brought was waiting on the coffee table. The room still smelled like him. I looked behind me, expecting to see Harvey trot to the recliner. But he wasn't here either.

So this was what it felt like to be lonely.

I sunk to the floor in front of the coffee table and pulled the wooden box toward me. It was made of polished wood, and the lid was slippery in my hands. Inside was a small pile of newspaper clippings—obituaries—and photos. I pulled a couple of the obituaries out and looked at the names. Nigel Pickering, one of the twins, was there. It was yellowed with age, almost thirty years old. Herbie Caldwell was there too, and I snorted with surprise when I read who his wife was—Sylvia Pickering, little Sylvia. I looked at the one on top. The strip of paper was still white and so long, it unfolded like an accordion.

The obituary was only a few weeks old. The photo was of a woman standing in front of an easel. Her hair was completely white and hung in a long braid over her shoulder. Even in the black and white photo, Bertie's personality shone through.

The obituary read:

Roberta "Bertie" Dorothy Johnston
(nee Gamache)

Born of humble beginnings on a farm in Saskatchewan, Bertie never let anything slow her down. Orphaned at a young age, she made her way west, first to Edmonton and then to Vancouver, where she earned a living as a housemaid and then as a waitress at a local coffee shop. She eventually took over ownership of the coffee shop and opened five more locations, all in down-town Vancouver. She married a customer, Stanley Johnston, and had two sons. Bertie loved life. She was an artist, a traveler, a music-lover, and a social butterfly. She

retired to the West Coast and woke up ev-
ery morning to a seaview. She is survived by
her two sons, Walter—

I couldn't read any more. My tears blurred so the letters swam together. She'd named her son after him.

"She forgave you," I say out loud.

I hoped that wherever Mr. Pickering was, he could hear me.

Chapter 41

Harvey

Harvey, the little white dog who started this story, is back at home with his Maggie. He is perfectly content. The days he was away from Maggie are a foggy memory now.

But every so often, when they're out for a walk, he'll catch the scent of an old pair of leather slippers, and he'll be reminded of a gnarled, trembling hand stroking his back. He will remember the musky, sweaty smell of the boy who cared for him. He will remember that he was happy there too. It was a place where he was loved.

And it was a place that, for a little while, he called home.

Acknowledgments

My first thanks go to my uncle, Wayne Pickering, who is the keeper of our family stories. After years of careful research, he has pieced together the history of the Pickerings, my grandpa's family. When *Harvey Comes Home* was a wisp of a book, I sent him an email asking if he knew of any stories about my grandpa and dogs. He replied right away with a story about General, a three-legged dog who chased away horse thieves from my grandpa's farm. This story became the centerpiece of Walter's childhood memories. I can't thank Uncle Wayne enough for remembering and sharing these treasures with me. He was also an early reader of *Harvey Comes Home*, and provided lots of historical notes and fact checking. That being said, any mistakes are my own.

In order to get the story of life in the prairies during the 1930s as accurate as possible, I relied on research. Two excellent books about this time period recommended by Wayne were Gerald Friesen's *The Canadian Prairies* and *Happyland* by Curtis McManus. I also spent a winter break grilling my in-laws about life on their farms when they were kids. Thanks to William Rae Nelson and Arlene Nelson for sharing their memories with me.

My biggest thanks go to Ann Featherstone, editor extraordinaire. Without her vision and insights, *Harvey Comes Home* would have stayed lost. She saw something in the manuscript I sent to Pajama Press and helped craft this sweet book into something so much better. I am immensely proud of the result.

Everyone at Pajama Press has been a pleasure to work with. Thank you especially to Gail Winskill for her leadership, warmth, and expertise. The book came together thanks to Erin Alladin, John Rowntree, Laura Bowman, Lorena Gonzalez Guillen, and Rebecca Bender. And Harvey came to life thanks to Tara Anderson's wonderful illustrations.

Finally, my little Westie (who was named Maggie) is still missed. Anyone who has loved a dog will understand the heartbreak of losing one. *Harvey Comes Home* is for her too.

An author and elementary school teacher, **Colleen Nelson** earned her Bachelor of Education from the University of Manitoba in her hometown of Winnipeg. Her previous novels include *Sadia*, winner of the 2019 Ruth and Sylvia Schwartz Award, and *Blood Brothers*, selected as the 2018 McNally Robinson Book of the Year for Young People. Colleen writes daily in between appearances at hockey rinks and soccer fields in support of her two sports-loving sons.

A folk artist and award-winning illustrator who trained at the Ontario College of Art and Design, **Tara Anderson** is known for her lively and humorous illustrations of animals. Her books include *Rhino Rumpus*, the award-winning *Nat the Cat Can Sleep Like That*, and her new picture book *Pumpkin Orange, Pumpkin Round*, featuring a family of charming cats celebrating Halloween. Tara shares a farmhouse in Tweed, Ontario with her husband, her young daughter, and several cats.